The Curious Adventures of Christian Carrick-Bentley

B. S. Davies

Published by B. S. Davies, 2017.

THE CURIOUS ADVENTURES OF CHRISTIAN CARRICK-BENTLEY

B S DAVIES

---

1. http://www.smashwords.com

THE CURIOUS ADVENTURES OF CHRISTIAN CARRICK-BENTLEY

First edition. March 10, 2017.

Copyright © 2017 B. S. Davies.

ISBN: 979-8227475671

Written by B. S. Davies.

To anyone daft enough to read this and appreciate it.

Day 21

My new escape has been foiled yet again when the guards discovered the start of "Cuthbert", my third tunnel. It was thwarted when the meagre scraping on the granite tiles of the floor of my cell caused by the sharpened aglet of the shoelace holding my left trainer together. I must admit that it was my fault; the lack of sleep due to attempting to escape every night since I was imprisoned is taking its toll and resulted in my snoozing during the repetitive scratching of the honed plastic end of my lace and my gentle snoring which aroused the guards to my attempt. But I was rather hoping that my guard, a staunch royalist, would be distracted by the impending Royal Birth, but alas, no.

I have, however, hatched another cunning ploy during my stints in the exercise yard (or as more fortunate beings would call it, "walking the dog"). It will involve a great deal of forward planning but will be worth it if it comes to fruition. With the imminent arrival of the second offspring of the Royal couple there will be the inevitable speculation and wagering on the name of the progeny of which I will not partake due to my total lack of success of picking the name of the third in line to the throne (I chose the names "size bed" and "prawn balls", which I thought would really come into their own once he became king). Then whilst my wardens are distracted by visiting the local Ladbrokes, I will pounce.

I digress.

My next daring attempt at escape will be to paint myself to resemble the bars of my cell and slowly edge toward the main gate; this may take quite a while to achieve discharge as I calculate the distance will take at least 17 weeks to traverse undetected, hampered, as it will be, by the necessity of returning to my cell every night so that my sentries do not realise what I am doing.

I must go now, it is the exercise minute and I must hide this paving slab and the piece of burnt candlewick that I am using to transcribe these events before they are discovered and confiscated and I have no wish to be nailed to the wall by my tongue as a punishment again.

I remain yours and forever hopeful.

Day 27

I have diligent tailored a complete body suit from my mattress liner and by wearing it when the team of three trustees who have been designated as the painting and decorating team refurbished my cell. I bribed them with two partially masticated Weetabix and gently cajoled them with the promise of an unopened catering sachet of tomato flavoured Cup-a-Soup into painting the back side of it to appear as the bars of an empty cell and the front as a plain brick wall (perfectly square and nicely pointed, none of that cowboy rubbish thank you very much).

On Day 24 I tested the efficacy of the suit by donning it and standing with my back to the bars to the left of my cell door just before the new guard, Miguel, came to check on me first thing in the morning. Success!

Miguel ran from the block shouting that I had escaped, and during the ensuing fuss and bother I quickly removed the suit and hid it under my mattress in the specially carved hidey hole. When Santiago, the most senior and most sceptical of my guards entered I was reclined upon my bed reading my oft thumbed copy of Canterbury Tales and I acted most bemused as Santiago berated the poor Miguel over his inefficiencies as a Prison Warder.

Yesterday I tested the front of the suit, again with the hapless Miguel on duty I stood with my back to the wall to appear as part of it. Once again he ran out shouting of my apparent absconding and once again when returning with Santiago I was found to be lounging on my bed reading the aforementioned classic by Chaucer. Further haranguing of poor Miguel supervened and with such gusto I almost felt sorry for the lad; but only almost.

During our extra-curricular activities last evening (three and a half minutes in the exercise yard attempting to dodge a torrent of high powered water issuing from the mouths of extremely compressed armadillos) I was able to smuggle my suit out by wearing it under my overalls and after successfully evading the water I stripped of my regulation prison garb and stood against the wall and disappeared! I thought it prudent to edge only one brick width at a time as to avoid detection, which seemed to work for the few hours it took me to creep toward the main gate. Then all hell broke loose.

Miguel was on the night shift, which was why I had decided to time my bid for freedom now; he once again ran helter-skelter from the prison block screaming of my escape, however, not unlike the boy who cried wolf, he was not believed. So incensed by the lack of response from his fellow Warders he proceeded to attack them with the blunt end of a felt-tipped pen that he had discovered on the floor of the recreation room that very afternoon.

By the time the furore had died down and Miguel had been forcibly removed in restraints I had reached the barrier which blocked the exit of the yard and I had turned with my back on display to appear as the bars of the gate. This was most fortunate as Miguel was being gently nailed for his own protection to the exercise yard wall by the other guards and it would have been most ill-fated, and probably nigh-on impossible, to carry out my escape successfully with a prison guard nailed to the front of my suit.

Lady Luck was with me that night as I clung to the gate as one of the guards from outside came in to witness the rare sight of the tacking of a rookie sentry to the wall. However, by the time I had managed to complete my escape with no further disturbances that most fickle of females had deserted me completely.

The prison is located in a desolate and barren tract of land with only one road passing it. I managed to walk several miles before a 16 wheeled articulated truck and trailer appeared and I tried to flag it down to obtain transport to wherever it was destined.

However I had forgotten the I was still wearing my self-crafted once piece suit and the truck driver panicked and used his CB Radio to contact the prison to report that one of their cells had escaped and was travelling west on the main road.

My attempt at freedom was at an end.

I am now frantically scribbling this meagre record of my failed endeavour of egress from this dastardly existence whilst languishing in the deep, dark solitary confinement crater. I am using the pelt of a large rat, which was supposed to be my evening meal, by dipping the end of its tail in a pool of the unfortunate rodent's blood and writing by the dim light of a gibbous moon.

Who knows what tomorrow will bring?

I am scheduled to be dragged off to the office of the Prison Governess, Bessie MacTavish, first thing in the morning to be summarily punished for my escape; the best I can hope for is to be nailed against the wall next to Miguel but not, with a bit of luck, next to Santiago who has been suspended upside down from the wall by having his ankles riveted together and hung up with dried skins of puff adders. But at least we shall all be company for each other.

Day 29

I am happy to report that I am returned to my cell and the relative safety it offers. But the quiet has been pierced on several occasions by the screams of Santiago in the next cell. Although now the bloodcurdling shrieks have now subsided into a quiet self-pitying mewling I can record the horrors I have witnessed.

When I was dragged before Bessie MacTavish the Governess she had me cuffed by my hands and feet across her wrought iron headboard in her private quarters. Whilst strapped there I witnessed such acts of depravity performed by Ms MacTavish upon Santiago the Prison Guard that I could barely bring myself to watch.

One particular incident will forever be burned into my memory; it involved the insertion of a drinking straw into the scrotum of the unfortunate Santiago by way of an opening cut with a rusty cheese knife and Bessie gently inflating his scrotal sack by blowing in the straw. I can only imagine that she has totally misunderstood the common slang for the act of fellatio.

I quailed in the face of the horrors visited upon the unfortunate Santiago and could not but worry for the safety of my own manhood as I lay there fastened across the headboard, but thankfully help was at hand and from a very peculiar source.

The remainder of the Prison guards, all having at some point suffered the twisted manipulations of the Governess, have formed their own escape committee and mounted a rescue bid to release Santiago from the evil clutches of Bessie, and finding me there as well decided, after a quick discussion lasting only a matter of hours, to release me also as they needed the handcuffs to restrain the Governess.

As I write this the Guards have barricaded themselves on the roof of the cookhouse along with the governess suspended on the headboard and have issued their demands to the authorities, they include the removal of the Governess, the reinstating of Rodrigues

Guevara, the previous Governor who was removed after it was rumoured that he was running an illicit Mexican Jumping Beans racket from the prison. They also demand longer coffee breaks and Pizza on Thursdays. This, however, has proved to be the sticking point of the negotiations; the Authorities offered Cheese toasties every other Wednesday, an offer that was met with derision and the threat of releasing Bessie in the offices of the Prison Authorities. This has now resulted in deadlock.

Hopefully this situation will resolve itself sooner rather than later and maybe even result in my release from incarceration so I can resume my life with the one I love and then start the fight to clear my name, once I have discovered why I was locked up in the first place.

Day 39

It's a day of celebration, Bessie is ill!

She caught an elegant bug which has infected the lower part of her extremities, so her left leg has swollen to the size of a tree and the right one has withered that of a twiglet. Apparently the wrought iron headboard that she had been fastened too had been rendered completely unsanitary due to her nefarious and sexually dubious actions upon the bed over the years.

Although it's not fatal, the doctor says that she could be out of actions for minutes!!!!

The Hispanic sector is rejoicing by taking over the rest of the prison and locking all Non-Hispanics into solitary confinement. Even now, as I scribbled these hurried note on my left arm in Pitman Shorthand to transcribe later, they are dragging me toward the 'Ball-pit of Redemption'; there they plan to hurl me to the bottom of it and leave me there for an undetermined amount of time. But at least I will be able to sort all the different coloured balls into some kind of order.

Day 137

For several weeks now the President Fred - ists have been barricaded in the Gym block whilst taunting the Hispanic sector by parading various items from the body building equipment passed the windows and hanging their favourite skipping ropes from the gutters.

I cannot, for the life of me, believe that the Incumbent President Frederick Manuel Ortega ever envisaged such a fallout from his election promise of an amnesty for all prisoners.

The first mutterings of discontent came from the 58 new prison guards brought in by the new governor, they did not want to lose their jobs almost instantly and went on strike. During the first hour of the withdrawal of labour 13 prisoners escaped, which rather defeated the point of the exercise.

Although heavily armed and with the demeanour of Mike Tyson on steroids (which is just a rumour), the choice of not shooting anyone looting the prison was not applied: for which I will be eternally grateful for as my cell is now decorated with a rather nice tapestry liberated from Bessie's boudoir, and a high definition home entertainment centre unshackled from the private quarters of the prison Chaplain; I was able to trade his 5 years subscription to "Hot Blonde Action" viewing card for HD DVD's of 'It's a Wonderful Life' and 'As Good As It Gets', with the promise of the new 'Stars Wars' movie which, unlike me, should be released soon.

I am now lying recumbent whilst recovering from routing two miles of cabling to enable electricity and 24hr television in my cell on the very Chaise-Lounge on which Bessie tortured Jose Cattrall; the Pet Strangler, to near death. I am sipping a perfectly chilled glass of Lucozade from the wine cooler kindly donated to me by Cyril Von Clout, the Baby Mangler, upon his death bed; I was so overcome by his generosity that I nearly took my hands from his throat.

If my release is not imminent, then at least I can watch 24 hours Sky News and let it regale me with its reporting that either too much sunshine is bad for me or the certainty that the world is proceeding downward in a handcart faster than anyone could imagine: but life will be OK because I can buy a new Juicer from Wilkinsons, Poundstretcher, Debenhams or any other decent department store. This make the five day hike up onto the roof with the 9 metre satellite dish strapped to my back almost worth it.

NEWSFLASH.

I have just received notification, via carrier hamster, that the provisional arm of the 'Salvation of the English Language' have taken over the Prison Tattoo Parlour and are subversively tattooing quotes from Shakespeare and Churchill on the backs of members of the Hispanic faction, who are craving some kind of endorphin release not available through work outs denied due to the occupation.

There is hope yet!

Day 140

I think the Prison Chaplain, Monsignor Albert Chaplain, laced my latest supply of Lucozade in an act of revenge for my swapping his weekly subscription to 'Readers Wives' for one for the Radio Times. It appears that over his years of ministering to the low life incarcerated here has given him contacts in the illicit Columbian Markets and he is using that to good effect against me.

Last night, a quiet balmy evening only interrupted by the occasional whimper of the 'Employee of the day' hanging from the skipping ropes above the gym, and after a particularly invigorating session of QI and Question Time, I cracked open a bottle from my new delivery and helped myself to two glassfuls of the energising refreshment.

Twenty minutes later I was backed into the corner of my cell trying to hide from the two seven foot rather aggressive pink rabbits wearing Stetsons who had suddenly appeared and started singing "Home on the Range" in the reggae style of one Mr. Robert Marley. Which, it transpired, was in reality only the return of Diego, my homing hamster bearing a message from the Hispanic prisoners asking me to record a popular Spanish soap opera which roughly translates into English as "Your Cousin Killed My Donkey, Now Wash my Dishes", I think.

So this morning, as you can probably imagine, I have a rather annoying and painful ache inside the back of my skull. That, and the Wailers humming "Old Man River" going around and around in my mind.

As my ailment clears I am formulating a plan to exact my own revenge, which will certainly involve three week old herrings, a length of red twine and an old Bontempi keyboard. But applied with great cunning and vigour it will result in an act of vengeance not seen since the days of Al Calpol, the gangster who ran the illicit baby soother market on the West Coast of America in the early 1940's!

It may seem a bit of an over-reaction on my part, especially to you who have only ever seen me lounging in the perfectly manicured gardens of my mansion while several servants tend to our every whim; or laughing gaily as we playfully knock a shuttlecock over the badminton net whilst sipping perfectly chilled Moet & Chandon. But this existence is gruelling, especially I have no idea why I was incarcerated nor for how long.

I am a changed man, but still undauntedly yours.

Day 141

I am, at the time of writing this, staring at poor Diego, my homing hamster, whom I have had to weld into his little Hamster Globe®.

I discovered that the main reason for the glut of communication with the Hispanic section of the prison was because Manuel O'Reilly, the Manic Yak Strangler of Cadiz, who has been driven mad by repeated self-gratification, has developed an affection for Diego and was attempting sexual congress with my dear little rodent friend.

After I had sent a reply to yesterday's message, Diego did not return within the usual timeframe and I, by way of semaphore utilizing torn bed sheets and tea towels, contacted my inside man, Jose Zanhora, the Deranged Flamenco Murderer, to make enquiries as to what had happened to Diego.

My plucky little emissary was returned to me two hours later in a state of distress and dis-array.

After the gentle application of two splints, a tourniquet and a chilli poultice which I bound with several elastic bands, he rallied and was soon leaping about his little home (an elaborate construction of potato mashers and several vegetable strainers) with abandon.

It was therefore, I felt, necessary to take precautions to protect him from any further sexual advances from the Yak Strangler and I placed him in his little transparent globe and, with the aid of "Strongo Super Glue®" ("Glue anything to anything, guaranteed!®") and taking care not to get any on his fur, I incarcerated him.

Unfortunately he started running about the cell, banging into objects almost immediately and, before the super-strength bonding had set sufficiently, he had stuck himself to the inside of his little ball of fun. I cannot explain the sadness that I feel as I watch him now as, due to the cognitive restrictions of his tiny hamster brain, he still attempts to run about but just whizzes lopsidedly around my cell, the ball wobbling greatly and making him cross-eyed with dizziness. I must also admit, to my immense shame that his efforts do make me laugh.

So much so that I nearly halved the price of the admission tickets for the other inmates and prison guards. "Diego the Whirling Hamster®" has very quickly become the most popular form of entertainment since somebody soldered the Prison Cook to a raft of crackers and floated him in the swimming pool for eight hours.

I am making so much money that I have even been able to employ one of the lesser criminals (Eric Estoban, the criminal mastermind behind the fraudulent postage stamp licking fiasco) to clean my cell of hamster vomit between performances.

Day 145

It is with a sad heart that I have to document the passing of "Diego the Whirling Hamster®".

Having made a moderate fortune from his seventeen performances per day, I could see the toll it was taking on my dear little rodent friend. I asked Eric Estoban if he could take a break from the cleaning of hamster bile to facilitate the gentle release of Diego from his Hamster Globe® and gently ease him with as little force as possible (as to not leave too much fur behind and reduce the resultant bald patch in case of photo opportunities) from the plastic wall on which he had bonded himself.

Estoban however, due to his lack of English, misunderstood me and took the globe to the workshop and proceeded to employ an oxy-acetylene welding torch to try and achieve the freedom of my plucky little hamster pal.

Words fail me as I attempt to describe the carnage this caused.

Not only did this action cause the total immolation of poor unfortunate Diego but manage to set fire to the entire workshop which also resulted in several fatalities within the Swedish Troupe of prisoners who were rehearsing their traditional Pickled Herring Polka, which is performed normally in the town of Tallberg by the shores of Lake Siljan.

However it is not all bad news, the newly appointed Prison Warden, Raul Cortez, attended the funeral of Diego the ex-Whirling Hamster® and has started calling me "Bastardo" which is a vast improvement on the traditional greeting here which is normally a blow to the back of the head with an oversized toffee hammer. This is surely in recognition that I am now the richest man in this correctional facility.

I have also started the intensive training, despite the complaints of the 'facción de Liberación Animal' of the North Wing, of "Alfonse the Messenger Mouse®" as a performing matchbox juggler.

Day 149

Woke up this morning cursing Chaplain Chaplain, my head felt like it had been turned inside out, rubbed down with emery cloth and soundly scrubbed with a stiff broom then turned the right way around with a baby hedgehog inserted. My Lucozade must have been drugged again.

I gingerly arose from my divan only to discover that I did not recognise my surroundings at all; gone were all the trappings of my recent success; my 56" HD television with surround sound, the three piece leather suite, the SMEG American Style fridge with my supply of beverages and, worst of all, my extensive collection of coloured Patagonian wool samples!

Had I been robbed during my drug induced slumber?

No! On further examination I discovered that I was in an entirely different cell, not only that, it was an entirely different prison!

The onset of panic was imminent when Facundo Hortez, the Prison Governor entered the alien cell. He explained that I had been moved to a new prison because death threats from the Hispanic sect had been issued against me and I had been sent here, Hernandez Cortina Open Prison, for my own safety and that all my prized possessions were being delivered this morning and were going to be tastefully arranged in my new luxury cell by Hernadez Muebles the convicted Interior Designer (his crime, roughly translated, was something to do with two rent boys, a vice and a herring). Until then, as a "highly valued personage" I would be allowed to spend the day in his plush quarters on the edge of the exercise yard, there, if I so wished, I could partake of perfectly chilled Lanson Black Label Champagne whilst idly flicking small ball bearings at lesser convicts as they were dragged around the yard by a forty year old tractor for their own wellbeing.

He also informed me that he had personally assembled a small group of staff for me, including a professional trainer to continue the preparation of "Alfonse the Messenger Mouse®" in his role as a matchbox juggler. Alfonse, I was informed, was currently thriving in a large disinfected cage which had only recently been vacated by "Bertrand the Dancing Chinchilla®" whose tragic loss was still mourned at the prison and the smoke from one of his graves could still be observed from the veranda where the champagne was on offer. A large marble mausoleum for the mortal remains of "Diego the Whirling Hamster®" was being constructed nearby by a group of disgruntled Icelandic prisoners.

After a large part of the day had been idled away imbibing Champers and managing only to partially blind three prisoners, I was informed that my cell was ready and awaiting my approval. I was stunned when I entered my new large abode (for how long this would be my erstwhile home, I still had no inkling), the whole place had been tastefully decorated with chintz wallpaper and satin swags which complimented the suite perfectly and it looked a perfect space to while away my indefinite incarceration. My musing was interrupted however, by my personal assistant, Boris Enfantica, the Mongrel Smotherer; a small ineffectual man with a habit of snorting through his left nostril which made him sound like he was sniggering at the most inopportune times (his right one was missing due to an unfortunate incident with a small puppy when he was three years old, hence his crime spree). He told me, between exhalations, that my vast fortune had arrived from my old habitation, and would I like to oversee the safety precautions as it was safely stashed away.

I had diligently counted my hoard of wealth, seventeen hundred boxes of Benson & Hedges, three hundred John Players, thirty of Rothmans, a packet of TUC biscuits and, most valuable of all, an inflatable Minion figure (am I the only one who thinks they look like lemon flavoured tic-tac's?); all safely delivered by CASH (Convict Assets Safely Handled), and was now observing employees of Secured Acquisition of Fortunes Ensured (SAFE) as they piled them into several dozen safety deposit boxes before sealing the three foot thick stainless steel combination locked door on the walk-in strong room which had been purposely installed behind my bed.

It may seem to you that I have very rapidly become a disciple of Croesus; but this apparent mindless pursuit of wealth does have an ultimate goal.

If I can become the wealthiest prisoner in the history of this country then my power will grow; so much so that the command of the relevant Authorities will be undermined and they will have to release me to regain their supremacy once more.

Day 153

My carefully laid machinations are undone!

This morning, whilst I was counting my fortune in the open strong room, "Alfonse the Messenger Mouse®" exploded whilst attempting to juggle with five matchboxes (a new world record for juggling mice, I am reliably informed), setting fire to all my wealth. Hernandez Jose Kinnear, his specialist trainer and expert felonious monastic purloiner, had decided to let the minute rodent train in my cell for the day as the diminutive rat had rather taken a shine to me and rebelled at the idea of his training taking place in the special converted gymnasium in the next block.

Unfortunately in the relocation of the equipment to my cell, Kinnear had forgotten to check all the Swan Vesta boxes used in training and, alas, one of them was full of unstruck matches. We suspect sabotage and the weight of suspicion falls fully on both members of the itinerant Icelandic faction who were, I believe, acting out of revenge for being commandeered to build the Mausoleum.

However all is not lost, I managed to rescue the inflatable Minion which only suffered minor smoke damage and a singed left arm. However, the heat has caused some damage to his appearance and when he is fully inflated he does resemble a jaundiced John Merrick.

But I am assured that everything is covered by my LEMMING (Life Ensuring for Mouse Manipulation of Inflammables, Napalm or Gunpowder) policy which I insisted on taking out against Alfonse with El Viva Insurance when I started this venture and I await the promised large cheque in the post.

In the meantime it has become incumbent on me to exact a revenge upon the Icelanders and I believe that I have a suitable plan.

Tonight, at the stroke of twenty seven minutes past ten, they will both be invited out to the exercise yard by Alberto Descarges, the Captain of the Guard, to witness a live interpretation of the Aurora

Borealis by the visiting Performance Group – "Las Mejores Reformas", and, as the Icelanders have professed to be immensely homesick, they should accept the offer immediately. They will be pounced upon by the impermanent arm of the Mongolian Yak Liberation Front.

Once he has used the remainder of my super glue to secure them to a hastily constructed 1.27th scale balsa wood model of the General Belgrano, I will set into motion a simple torture technique taught to me by my Nepalese Sherpa, Roger, one July morning as we awaited the arrival of the narrow gauge railway carriage for a particularly treacherous assent to the summit of Mount Snowdon.

It involves the subtle application of several kitchen implements and, due to the popularity of Alfonse, the kitchen staff have gladly donate brand new equipment some of which are even still in their packaging.

I will report on the result in tomorrow's missive.

Day 154

The best laid plans.....

All the preparations to exact my revenge made last night came to nought, when the Icelandic pair, Vincent Odinger, the Polar Bear Baiter, and Klaus Chong, the infamous half Chinese half Danish Oxo cube rustler, did not show up for the seminal performance of "Luz de la Norte" by Las Mejores Reformas.

It transpires that Alphonse exploding was an important element of an elaborate plan to facilitate the escape of the Scandinavian scoundrels who used the concert as a distraction to utilize the tunnel they had excavated under the Mausoleum during its construction.

They should not get very far. Prison Governor Hortez informs me that this prison is actually on an island thirteen miles from any mainland and located directly in the centre of a major migration route for half the world's sardine population which attracts many oceanic predators, so unless the "Icelandic Ingrates", as they have been named, have some kind of boat; which is highly unlikely, then any attempt of escaping the island is futile.

But until they are apprehended and repatriated into the prison, I should not dwell on their punishment, there are more pressing matters to attend to; the replacement of "Alfonse the Messenger Mouse®".

I arranged for the newly converted rodent gym to be available for the auditioning for the position previously occupied by my money spinning rodent. The line of applicants stretched for inches.

After an exhaustive afternoon of enduring dozens of animals, some talented and some not so, I had reduced the possibilities to four:

Graham the Gecko who could regurgitate variously coloured locusts he had ingested in the order that was chosen at random;

Malcolm the counting Sloth who could tap out the number shown on two rolled dice (unfortunately it took three hours for him to count out a six and a four),

And a rather overweight Siamese cat called Shona who could bite the tops off cola bottles and not lose too many teeth in the process.

Of the four that had made this shortlist my favourite was a team of seven hummingbirds, owned by Gomez Gomez, the Puppy Worrier from Maracaibo. He had trained them, by means of clipping varying numbers of small plastic staples on their wings, to hum particular notes in the scale of C and so, by carefully administering a small electric shock from an AAA battery, he could induce them to play "The Belles of St. Mary's" or "Edelweiss"; unfortunately, to ensure that his team won he embarked on a, some would say, over-elaborate hummingbird rendition of Bohemian Rhapsody which facilitated the necessity for a specialist aviary resuscitation team having to be called after a nasty accident with two of the diminutive birds collapsing during the operatic section. They were successfully revived by the cautious application of a reduced compound of my Lucozade with a small syringe.

I now have to enter into carefully considered negotiation with Gomez Gomez for the acquisition of "Humm!"

Day 156

Well I talked that up did I not?

It appears that the Icelandic duo on the run have both found ways off this godforsaken lump of rock.

Vincent Odinger, the Polar Bear Baiter, made it to the west coast and dove into the balmy current of the South Sea Temperate Stream which flows toward the equator, the very channel of warm water in which the sardines follow. He was able to attract the attention of a passing sardine canning boat, which, by all coincidences, turned out to be a decommissioned Icelandic Gunboat once used in the "Cod Wars" between his Motherland and the United Kingdom in the cold waters north of Scotland in the 1970's.

Klaus Chong found his way to the south where, as conveniently forgotten by Prison Governor Hortez, there appears to be the "Timbuctoo Hotel and Holiday Complex" which has been operating on this island for several years and boasts a water park, 3d cinema and a cluster of well know food chains as well as a four star hotel. Apparently it just "skipped" Hortez's mind; I will have to have a word with that man.

I digress.

Chong was able to gain access to the holiday cruiser "Conchita" which has been in port for two days before setting off back to the Mediterranean. He boarded her under the pretence of being a stranded member of a Chinese Male Voice Choir, the other members having been transported by a ship from Hong Kong whilst he had been left behind because of his dissident attitude. They disembarked only an hour after Chong had boarded.

However the Fickle Finger of Fate pointed its indiscriminate digit at the unfortunate pair at that moment. Sven Willeyebefamous the owner/skipper of the fishing vessel and veteran of the Cod Wars suffered a grand mal brainstorm and mistook the cruiser "Conchita" for a British trawler and fired the last remaining torpedo at her.

The projectile, which had lain dormant in its launch tube since the mid 70's, was not in its prime condition and prematurely detonated as it left the metal cylinder it had called home for over forty years blasting a large hole in the fishing vessel "Olga". A tragic chain of events then followed; the disremembered and therefore neglected ammunition magazine below decks on the starboard side reacted to the explosion and ignited as the boat passed closely to the port side of the holiday cruiser, sending both vessels plunging to the bottom of the ocean.

Sven and his eight strong crew were all able to reach the Olga's lifeboat safely. The crew and passengers of the Conchita, including Chong, were in the water for the best part of an hour, successfully beating off several attacks by the sharks which had been circling the shoals of migrating sardines, before all were rescued by a passing Chinese Cargo ship. Once on board the Captain of the cruiser introduced Chong to the commander and he is now, apparently, below decks on his way to Taiwan to be shot as a deserter and subversive.

Meanwhile, the rehearsal for "Humm!" are proceeding well after my successful negotiations with Gomez Gomez when the financial concerns were settled rather easily as he accepted the disfigured inflatable Minion (Gomez is a big fan of the David Lynch film "The Elephant Man", who would have guessed?) and a three percent share in the profits for the first four shows. Things progress well...

Day 158

The opening night of "Humm!" was an unmitigated disaster.

The fifty minute delay in the curtain going up was acceptable, given that we were dealing with performing creatures and their needs were paramount; but if I ever catch the son of an unnamed father who laced their nectar with hallucinogenic drugs I will not be responsible for my actions. Thankfully, in a twisted way, my second director, Hector was mildly addicted to sugar and if it had not been for him taking a hit from the glass feeder before fitting it into the cage holding our diminutive stars, we would never have known until it was too late. Had he not started proclaiming that "Everything is so green!" it could have been show over before it had even started. But, given what happened next, that may have been for the best.

The first act went without a hitch, even the tricky passage from "Jupiter: the Bringer of Joy" from the Planet Suite by Gustav Holst went without a single error. But, alas and alack, the second act dissolved into chaos very quickly indeed when the small paper clips on the wings of the hummingbirds, loosened, it would appear, by the rendition of the 1812 Overture performed just before the interval, rapidly started to part company with their feathered appendages and fly across the stage.

Although these items of stationary were made of pliant plastic and very small, they were travelling at a much accelerated rate due to the high speed vibrations of the hummingbird wings. Too miniscule to directly cause damage to anybody they came into contact with, the sensation at impact resembled the sting of a wasp but that was enough to cause a reflexive action, which in an enclosed area such as the prompting pit where I was enclosed with second director Hector was enough to cause total chaos.

Hector was extremely allergic to wasp stings, so when he was struck on his forehead by a paperclip he assumed the worst and panicked completely. In his state of complete and utter dread he leapt upon the stage by way of the handle which releases the fire curtain in the event of catastrophe; ironically it was this in itself which caused the tragedy. The weighted curtain dropped with speed and trapped poor Director Hector by his extremely long nasal hair it was at that point the elephants, which were to be used in the finale with a rendition of Count Basie's "Carnival", stampeded from stage right; a course of action that left him less of three dimensional form than he had been only moments before.

Poor Hector, he will be missed, but at least the sugar ration will increase.

Although, on a happier note, more tickets are being sold now, plus I have saved three percent of the takings and had my inflatable Minion returned!

Day 160

It was the funeral of Second Director Hector today.

A sad occasion, made doubly so because it was also the collective funerals of the four members of "Humm!" who tragically lost their little lives in the carnage that ensued during the second act of the first night performance.

A, D, F# and G were laid to rest side by side in a ceremonial shoebox on the sunny side of Diego the Whirling Hamster's Mausoleum, whilst Hectors interment took place in the skip at the back of the cookhouse. Some inmates are saying it was a slight to the memory of Hector, but really it was just an administrative error due to his surname – Nectar-Rivour, which, by complete coincidence, is the classification for creature who live on the sugary sap of flowers. Unfortunately, the error which had caused the dumping of the flattened corpse of Second Director Hector Nectar-Rivour did not come to light until an hour after the local refuse collecting truck had paid its daily visit.

A prison van was dispatched almost immediately with several close friends of Second Director Hector Nectar-Rivour to try and reclaim his mortal remains; that was several hours ago now and the van has still not returned. I can only surmise that they are rummaging through the refuse at the tip of 10,000 hectare for Second Director Hector Nectar-Rivour on the west side of the Island.

It is almost midnight and the other hummingbirds have settled now after, what I can only surmise was a Trochilidae style lament for their dearly departed which had lasted for three hours. They have all now thankfully slipped into their habitual state of almost hibernation, until their first nectarivous meal tomorrow morning.

The guards from the van dispatched to try and retrieve the remains of Second Director Hector Nectar-Rivour have returned sans transport. The friends of the late impresario took the opportunity and escaped on a Russian refuse barge whose Captain gladly accepted the prison transport as payment.

The search begins tomorrow for the replacements for the main line up of "Humm!"...The show must go on!

Day 164

After an exhaustive search for the replacements to the line-up of "Humm!" I think we may have succeeded. My new second director, an ex- medical man convicted of mal-practice, Victor Proctor to replace Second Director Hector Nectar-Rivour has been of great assistance.

But it was not all plain sailing however, we had to plough our way through seventy five auditions in three hours to whittle down the possibilities to five:

Malcolm the Merganser Duck who produced a low pitch hum through the rapid vibration of his bill, but it caused a bit of a stir as it was discovered that it was the precise frequency of the Captain of the Guard, Alberto Descarges' new spectacles when they exploded during a snap inspection of the orchestra pit. It was fortunate for him that Second Director Victor Proctor is a Doctor and was able to save the poor man's left eye; although the right one (providentially a glass one) is still missing, but I and several other people believe that a search of Fidel O' Reilly, the Morbidly Obese Cat Burglar's cell may reveal its whereabouts.

Connie the Performing Goldfish; she swims around her large tank and is able to indicate the name of anybody she can see: as long as their name is Robert, awkwardly, she did not survive the audition when her tank exploded the same time as Alberto's glasses.

Frederick the Bolivian Screaming Hairy Armadillo, who, once shaved and handled correctly emits a pitch perfect f#.

Beauregard the Chilean Alpaca who spits at strategically placed dinner gongs of varying notes to produce tunes.

And, Clement the Yellow-tailed Woolly Monkey, who sadly, is tone deaf; but, because he is one of the rarest creatures of South America and found only in the mountainous area of northern Peru, does not really have to do anything to attract onlookers.

This is a very important decision as the Governor has mooted the fact that we may be able to perform "Humm!" at the nearby "Timbuctoo Hotel and Holiday Complex".

Day 170

I am hastily scribbling this on the back of a scrap from a nautical chart of the South China Seas in a relatively calm five foot swell somewhere in the South Atlantic whilst huddled in the hold of a tramp steamer heading to heaven knows where.

I have escaped!

I had planned to chart this course of action very carefully over the next few weeks as the performances became more and more popular with the tourists at the Hotel; however I had to bring my strategy to bare almost immediately. You will understand the necessity when I tell you that the Governor was replaced unexpectedly, more than likely due to the unprofessional, and probably unconstitutional, deference he was showing to me and a certain few other inmates in return for financial gain. Removed, not because he was corrupt, but because none of his ill-gotten advantages ever made it higher up the food chain. But I wander off course (to use a nautical turn of phrase), he was replaced by none other than Bessie MacTavish!

She is out of intensive care and the half of her face which had been inadvertently chewed away by a swarm of soldier ants and a desperately starving seagull whilst she was chained to her own headboard on the roof of the cookhouse. It has been temporarily replaced by a carefully fashioned papier-mâché mask which gives her the appearance somewhat of a cardboard Phantom of the Opera, I think it's the cloak.

She recognised my name in the prison records and demanded immediately that I was brought to her. Fortunately I was at the Hotel putting the final touches to the inaugural public performance of "Humm!" and the message was passed to Second Director Victor Proctor, the Doctor, during Beauregard the Chilean Alpaca's solo from the overture of "Chitty Chitty Bang Bang" and it gave me palpitations I can tell you.

Fortunately I have formed a very close profession relationship with the Timbuctoo Hotel and Holiday Complex's General Manageress, Ms Genevieve Seymour Fanworthey, whom, it transpires, knows my cousin, Cedric Comely-Nightly, the fourth Duke of Reigate, as she personally comforted him during the dreadful allegations about his romantic antics with a morally questionable Cayman Crocodile collector from Dorset and several damp copies of Duchess of Mozambique's Last Will and Testament, which appeared in that dreadful gutter tabloid the Swanage Weekly News. The allegations were proved to be totally unfounded (she actually collected Nile Crocodiles) and an undisclosed sum of compensation was paid quietly to the Duke; apparently it was enough to keep him in Parma Violets for several weeks. So, upon hearing of my predicament and impending endless torture at the hands of Bessie, Ms Seymour Fanworthey agreed to hide me at the Complex.

I spent three days awaiting transport disguised as "Trumpeting Billy" the complex mascot, why an Elephant, the Lord only knows; but it involved me wearing an oversized and almost fluorescent orange rubber and polyester elephant suit. Not too bad as nobody could ever guess it was me, especially with the eight foot span ears and a four foot trunk encompassing a bugle and which I have only tripped over nineteen times, and only then ending up in one of the three swimming pools twice due to my natural agility! Plus the five octogenarian guests that I hospitalised in the process were quite understanding too. The dunking's were, I have to say, a welcome relief as the heat of these balmy summer days is amplified fivefold in the suit.

On the fourth day I bid a fond farewell to Genevieve and Second Director Doctor Victor Proctor, both of whom seem to have taken a shine to each other judging by the noise emanating from her room on the third night, and boarded my present home.

"The Zanzibar Kid", sailing under a Liberian flag of convenience and originally built in Dublin Dockyards in the early 1900's in the shadow of the construction of the Titanic, is an eighty foot, twin funnelled steamer plying its trade between Maracaibo, Cadiz and Lowestoft carrying cargo which its ebullient Captain, Tad Norris, refers to as "Products of Entertainment Value" but will not offer any further explanation aside from a tap on the side of his nose and a theatrical wink.

I did have a cabin just below decks, but as my happiness at this new found freedom culminated in my unconsciously whistling off-key whilst accompanying Radio Four's "Afternoon Theatre" and out of tune harmonising during "The Archer's" which emanate daily from the radio room next door, it was requested that I bunk near the bilge pumps. I do not mind at all when I tremulously think of the fate that would have engulfed me at the Prison; beside their rhythmic thump does send me into a dreamless sleep. It could be as little as four months before I am once again at your side! I cannot wait to caress your pearl-like neck and once again kiss the back of your left knee.

I hope this message finds you as I only have an over-stretched hair scrunchie with which to fasten it to the leg of Morris the Homing Stormy Petrel whom, it would seem from his struggles, is as eager to deliver it as I am for you to receive it.

Day 175

This sickness has been plaguing me for three days now. It is definitely not Mal de Mere because we are becalmed in the Doldrums; which is an accomplishment in itself as we are driven by four thirty-two cylinder diesel engines. Not so much of an accomplishment is preventing Curt Strangheim, the demented German Navigator from relieving himself in the fuel tank. I suggested locking the cap on the tank, but was overruled because I "am a landlubber" and "know nothing about life at sea".

I have decided not to tell them of my Great Uncle Geoffrey Under-Linguist who, whilst serving aboard HMS Ajax, personally vomited all through the Battle of the River Plate; and then went on to feel particularly queasy as they awaited for the Admiral Graf Spee to leave Montevideo.

Nor will I mention Admiral of the Fleet Montgomery Cleft, my Great Great Maternal Grandfather, who oversaw the disastrous engagement between HMS Guerriere and USS Constitution during early days of the American War of Independence through a hole in the tarpaulin covering the last lifeboat, as a safety precaution, of course.

Landlubber indeed!

My queasiness, unlike my Great Uncle's, I am sure was brought about by the strange looking comestibles served up thrice daily by Lok Goran the Zanzibar Kid's Sino-Portuguese cook. I am not one to complain, especially as he actually struggles all the way down here to my humble six foot square cabin with two trays of various items which always look as if they have been fed to the ship's cat (who died mysteriously yesterday), then regurgitated and fried in a sesame sprinkled teriyaki style batter and always tastes of week old cod and engine oil; but as it is the only source of sustenance on-board, I have no choice but eat it.

Apparently, the ships company did stage a revolt about the standard of cuisine eighteen months ago. But that course of action only led to Goran barricading himself in the galley and refusing to come out. The siege lasted for five days until the crew relented after they had eaten all the rats and started to feel a bit peckish.

I must leave you now as the need to evacuate my ravage stomach once more is overwhelming. Still; it's only the eighth time this morning...

Day 178

Tragedy has struck on board The Zanzibar Kid. Yesterday, Lok Goran, the ship's cook, overcome with remorse at causing my stomach upset, has thrown himself overboard.

He's not dead; he had the fortune and forethought to deploy the only lifeboat, complete with six weeks supply of bottled water and mini chocolate rolls before he leapt. I can hear his plaintiff screech of "So rong suckers!" as he rowed away whistling the theme from "Love Story" heading west by northwest as nobody batted an eyelid. So uninterested was the crew that nobody even suggested launching the intercontinental ballistic jellyfish that had been reserved for this very type of mutinous behaviour.

No, the tragedy is that I have been elected the new Ship's Cook. Me; the man who single handedly gave the entire third form of Irby upon Humber Public School dysentery by way of water that I had already boiled to rid it of impurities - twice.

But every cloud has a silver lining, and this particular cloud has three, Goran, in his rush to abandon ship, forgot his laptop computer with all his recipes on the hard drive AND an internet connection, also in his eagerness for decamping he also left half of his secret store of mini rolls along with, thirdly, a year's supply of Trex cooking fat and sesame flower based Teriyaki mix. So deep fried Swiss Rolls are on the menu for the next few days at least!

I have attempted set up a new email address to avoid spammers, I have been able to join a little-known server which caters for absolute fanatics of the BBC soap opera "EastEnders" (dot@dot.dot), it's all rather obscure, and I'm not really if the address will work, and even if it does I don't think our cache of Homing Stormy Petrol's will be too pleased and may embark on some subtle sabotage; they are already looking at me in funny ways.

Day 181

Captain Tad Norris, does not appear as ebullient as he seemed when I first boarded the Zanzibar Kid. In fact he has been behaving rather indecorously toward me and has used some terms of insult that I had to look up on Wikipedia to fully understand their import.

The thirty-seven strong crew of the Zanzibar Kid has dwindled to seventeen, which may account for the good captain's ill-mannered disposition toward me and my gastronomic endeavours. He compared my recipe to rancid Yaks milk; what opportunity he has had be in the vicinity of a rancid Yak, let alone had an opportunity to taste its milk I have no idea.

Even though I insisted that the demise of the twenty unfortunate matelots was due to a particularly virulent form of Dengue Haemorrhagic Fever transmitted by the large population of mosquito's who inhabit the lower section of the bilge; but the Captain insists, with a logic I cannot fault, that if it was so then I, as my accommodation is next to the colony of blood sucking insects, should have been the first infected.

My only excuse is that I am naturally immune to the attack of the minute plague carriers.

It has been proven, I have read, that the female mosquito are attracted by the emission of keriomones, a naturally occurring phase just caused by exhalation, but some people, approximately 20%, produce a chemical from their pores which masks their keriomones; and I just happen to be one of those people. The irate Captain then sought refuge in hurling insults of a most personal nature at me, which led me to conclude that either he may not have accepted my explanation; or I was correct in my assumption.

I went back to the galley because my Stormy Petrol Casserole could have started boiling over at any time. I must say it was fortunate that the ample supply of the birds was a godsend, especially when they started to drop down dead, foaming at the beak and having turned blue beneath what little feathers were left on the poor creatures, just as we ran out of Mini Rolls and sesame flour.

A quick rinse under the cold water tap and the remaining plumage just washes away (provided the poor misfortunate avian has been hung for a period not shorter than one day, but no longer than five), the yellowish foam coating gives up its vice-like grip on the beak after a good sharp scrub with a piece of emery cloth; then a skewer is inserted and they are hastily smoked over the embers of a smouldering wellington boot (which I found as a job lot in the corner of one of the cargo holds), then plunged into a boiling pan of seawater (this negates the use of adding salt) the resulting stew is not a particularly appetising colour, but then a drop of extract of cochineal does the trick and the taste is disguised with a large dollop of curry paste and a small spoonful of rancid Yak's milk. The supply of Petrol's is dwindling, but then again so is the crew, so it evens itself out really.

But I still have my reserve of two hundredweight of illegal wine gums to survive upon, and I have email now, so the aviary would be redundant anyway.

Day 184

It would appear that I am in the good books of the Captain once again!

Admittedly, he was delirious with a temperature of 132 degrees and kept calling me "Mother"; but he has promoted me to replace the ships navigator who passed away two evenings ago, which my cooking cannot be held responsible for as he was a vegetarian.

The promotion came after the recommendation of First Mate Rollo Aquifer, who had spotted me writing that note to you on the back of the chart and assumed that I could read maps. I have not got the heart to tell them that I even failed my Duke of Edinburgh Bronze Award for Orienteering when I guided my three companions to the edge of a cliff near Folkestone when we were only supposed to navigate our way from the school in Irby upon Humber to the town of Laceby just outside Grimsby, a distance of one and a half miles.

But I was happy to be out of the grubby little Ship's Galley, especially as the last meal I had concocted, Cornish pasties, were baked with pastry made from, what I though was a rather finely sifted, flour that I had obtained from the hold containing the "Items of Entertainment Value" that the Captain had referred to. This meal had been met by, not derision by the crew as normal, but rather they started laughing and joking. The Cabin Boy, Billy Groats, stood rather unsteadily and proclaimed his undying love for the ships cat and threw himself into the water. Fourteen of the other crew members though that was a rather good idea and joined him; what occurred then was a dreadful sight that will stay in my mind for a very long time, a large shoal of sunfish mistook them all for krill and mercilessly attacked them.

So now, with just a six strong crew of bowed, but brave men, and on deck with a view, I set about plotting a course of Northeast which would bring us to landfall on the west coast of Africa.

On the fifth day I was standing at the bow of The Zanzibar Kid along with the First Mate when I spotted a large raft of Emperor Penguins and remarked to Rollo that it was unusual to see them so far north and he mentioned that West Africa seem to be a lot colder that he remembered. It was then that we could make out the coastland in the distance and I could see what he meant as there seemed to be an awful lot of snow present for the Gabon, and that immense iceberg was getting damned close to the ship.

As the First Mate raced to the wheel house to avoid the oncoming frozen leviathan, I covertly shuffled to the map room to check on my course settings and to my dismay discover that, once again I had inverted the charts and we were actually approaching the coast of Antarctica! Fortune favours the brave, they say, however sometimes it favours raving cowards like myself; First Mate Aquifer, in his struggle to avoid the threat of a similar fate to the Titanic, turned the ship 180 degrees and in the process broke the only compass on the bridge.

So now the Zanzibar Kid is steaming on the correct course toward South Africa and Cape Town to take on provisions.

Day 194

So my course correction was a little off; but by my previous standards, it was very close. I write this from the town of Beira on the shores of the river Rio Púnguè in Mozambique, just south of the Zambezi Delta, as my clothes dry out.

They received a soaking when, due to my slight navigational error, we ended up missing Cape Town by a matter of a two hundred miles (which equated to only few degrees on a map) and found ourselves steaming toward Madagascar.

Fifteen miles south west of the island we were torpedoed by a French gunboat who mistook the Zanzibar Kid for a pirate raider, and our plucky little tramp steamer sank without a trace in a matter of moments. How the three of us made to the African coast I will never know. Billy Groats was taken captive by the French Navy and the other two of the remaining crew were lost at sea; so that just left Captain Tad (whose fever was somewhat reduced by our untimely dunking by our Gallic friends, but we still had to float him on a piece of the old aviary to prevent him drowning whilst he still insisted in calling me "Mother"), and First Mate Rollo.

With a fortuous tail wind, it only took us two days of swimming (and occasional splashing ineffectually to scare away a determined flock of over-amorous seagulls attracted by, presumably, the lingering smell of the Petrol's) to get to shore, where we met with laughter and the warm waving in our direction of various calibre weapons by the locals as we struggled over the sand with the now comatose Captain.

By way of compensation for the attack by "Marine nationale", Rollo and I find ourselves ensconced in the Hotel Miramar in the Ponta Gea with the compliments of the French Government, while the Captain is being treated at the local hospital for a combination of Dengue fever and malnutrition (so it was not my cooking after all!).

The next step of the journey will be to travel over land to Harare and find the British Consulate. The French Authorities have promised us transportation, so this stage should not take long!

I'll be home by the summer!

Day 200

Having spent the last few weeks sipping gin and tonics on the veranda of my hotel room (it's amazing; after four the smell from the nearby fish processing factory does not seem to be so bad, six or more who cares about the smell anyway?), whilst eating slices of fresh mango which i slice with a machete purchased at the local market. Rollo, the ex-First Mate of the Zanzibar Kid, has told me that he will not be travelling with me to Harare as he has found employ on an Illegal Norwegian Whaling ship as a blubber processor and he is leaving this afternoon.

I have never really been one for long farewells; so I patted him on the back and wished him "bon voyage", unfortunately I had forgotten that I was holding the machete in that hand and accidentally sliced most of the flesh from his upper back and the musculature of the top of his right arm, but he should be out of intensive care in a few weeks, and he is left handed anyway.

I have been informed that I travel to Harare tomorrow, but, due to budgetary demands the French Consulate here can only provide me with a thirty year old moped which has seen better days; but it is a choice of that, or walking the 300 plus miles.

I have chosen the motorised bicycle and I leave at five thirty tomorrow morning and I must now walk three mile round trip to the fuel depot with the two 10 gallon Jerry Cans I have been given for the journey as the 1 gallon tank is totally dry as this particular mode of transport has not been used for over a year and was previously propped up against the rotting corpse of a water buffalo around the back of the Hotel.

Never mind, it should make for an interesting trip!!

Day 201

I started this day with a great amount of trepidation as I prepared for my departure on my moped for the journey to Harare. I had supplies and water in a satchel which had been strapped to the front of me by the obliging Maitre'D of the Hotel restaurant, Geoffrey N'Dogo, and with one of the 10 gallon jerry cans secured to the back of me and the other, with a goose feather pillow placed on top serving as a saddle, I set off.

As I puttered and wobbled down the main road, the townsfolk gathered to wave me off and set about their traditional "Firing Indiscriminately at Anything That Moves" which seemed to happen frequently. Which I responded to by falling off twice and having to be helped back upright by several of the well-wishers.

Four miles north, in the town of Manga, the moped stopped for no apparent reason, but upon checking I discovered that the traditional farewell of the Townsfolk of Beira had resulted in one of the errant shots piercing the small fuel tank on the right hand side, which would have been an easy hole to repair, but the exit hole on the left of the tank had taken out most of that side. It is most fortunate, and totally inexplicable, how it managed to missed certain tender parts of my anatomy during its flight, suffice to say that if it had made contact I would be writing this in a high voice. The only reason that the fuel did not ignite was that the tank was so small it only held two pints at a time.

So I had to steel myself for a three hundred mile walk to Harare; at least I could dispose of the jerry can on my back. As I was extricating myself from the aforementioned fuel container a truck transporting salted fish, predominantly Bulawayo Baking Fish, pulled up and I managed to barter passage to the Capital of Zimbabwe as he was passing through on his journey to Bulawayo.

I write this account in the cabin of the fish lorry as we bump and jolt our way at a sedate twenty mile an hour toward the border. I am having to wear a complicated arrangement of a small lace handkerchief, two fairly clean socks and an old Aston Villa supporter's scarf dowsed in a very cheap cologne to cover the smell of rancid salted fish emanating from the rear of the truck. But at least I do not have to walk through, what I am reliably inform in pigeon English by my driver, is "dangerous grounding with many lians who eat peoples".

I just hope he knows where he is going and doesn't ask me to map read.

But do not despair I am getting closer, my love!

Day 202

The "Happy Valley Fish Supplies" truck in which I have been slowly but steadily travelling toward Harare broke down whilst approaching the border crossing between Mozambique and Zimbabwe in a pass between the Inyanga Mountains and the Vumba National Park.

The three of us; the driver Robert M'nobe, his companion Blessing Abango and myself have just had to unload the four and a half ton of salted Bulawayo baking fish so that Abango could gain access to mechanical parts of which I have no knowledge as the only terms for them were told to me in the native language by Blessing, who appears to be the more mechanical minded of my two travelling companions, and then translated by Robert who reliably informed me that the "Rod who makes truck go" had "becoming dislodged with gay abandonment" and required "most knocking of parts with big bangs".

Once Blessing had knocked most of the parts and with very big bangs which attracted not only a curious rhinoceros, but several of the border guards from the crossing a mile up the road, but seemed to do the trick. At the guards insistence, and gesturing at various parts of our anatomy with their Lee Enfield .303's and two AK 47's, we loaded the fish back into the truck PDQ and set off toward the border where the, now familiar, guards just waved us through with minor inquisitiveness as they had already divined that we really did not have anything of value, and we made our way toward the town of Mutare to refuel.

Once there, Robert and Blessing decided the "big bangs" had not been enough and they would take the opportunity to dismantle "Rod who makes truck go", so before they could ask me to once more unload their now extremely fragrant cargo, I decided that I would take a walk and see if I could find somewhere to take a bath.

I found a small tavern on the main road, and with a little fuss and a lot of hand signals which I thought were fairly representative of indicating my needs but were actually interpreted by the owner that

I was in desperate need of a lobster, a fire extinguisher, two shots of tequila and a witch doctor. This misunderstanding was overcome by the timely intervention of one of the two customers in the tavern, Christopher Manning, an author; the other customer was just called Sedgewick, according to Mr. Manning, but he said nothing and just sat at the bar stroking his pet Ocelot, Simon, barely acknowledging anyone else's existence except to indicate when he required another mint julep.

Christopher told me he was in Mutare researching the life of the British author Cecil William Mercer, who wrote under the nom de plume 'Dornford Yates' who had lived there until his death in 1960. I professed as to having never heard of the name. Manning then regaled me with facts about the writer; apparently he was a barrister and took an active part in the trial of Crippen, the notorious poisoner whilst finding time to write articles for Punch Magazine under his pen name which he derived from the surnames of both of his grandmothers, he also wrote a series of books called "Berry and Co." based in Edwardian England and mastered in novels which avoided reality and a changing world. I informed him that it sounded like my recent life and he became completely intrigued and asked me to relate my adventures, albeit in an abridged form; but I insisted that I was in desperate need of performing my ablutions first and he directed me to his rooms and gave me the key.

After a refreshing bath and a change of clothes provided by my new acquaintance, I returned to the bar where I began recounting my various catastrophes of the recent past in which Christopher was extremely interested. During my tales of woe, I rather over imbibed both of the ice cold bottles of lager with which my latest friend had provided and lost all track of time. Once I realised I stood, somewhat unsteadily as I had not drunk any alcohol since the leaving party of Antonia Trevallien the Italian-Cornish prison cook (and that had been brewed in the illicit still behind the library and was of a dubious concoction of waste products including rice, pasta and an indistinguishable vegetable matter); declaring I had to leave to continue my journey.

Manning offered to accompany me to the truck stop as I was unsure of the direction. After a short fifteen minute stagger we rounded the corner where the truck had been parked, but, alas, no sign of the "Happy Valley Fish Supplies" truck could be found, apart from the lingering smell of rancid Bulawayo baking fish.

I had been abandoned!

Day 204

In the light of a new day my predicament did not appear as bleak as it did yesterday.

My new friend Christopher Manning found me a room at the tavern and whilst I descended into an uneasy sleep in a surprising comfortable bed he booked passage for both of us on a train bound to Harare; the railway station not being very far from our accommodations. The route, he informed me over a light breakfast consisting of cornflakes and goats milk more akin to cheese (which I declined and ate a meagre fruit salad), would pass through the townships of Rusape and Marondera where he had to meet someone at the station there before continuing to the capital.

Over breakfast, and several cups of coffee, Manning took me into his confidence and told me that he was actually acting as an industrial spy for the Slobodov brothers, William and Benjamin, who were blackmailing him into stealing industrial secrets from the Horticultural Research Centre at Marondera. I ask of the nature of the blackmail, but he would not divulge much information except to mention an incident at Cambridge with a "Very Important Person" who became obsessed with some "French Poodles" and their owner which the inevitable dalliance became somewhat complicated when he came to be involved in a raid on the Huntingdon Animal Research Centre using a stick and a roll of "Wonder web".

I then enquired about the secrets he was attempting to obtain and offered my assistance in any way feasible. He thanked me for my offer and mentioned that it involve some rather exotic fruit, a secret formula which produced straight bananas and something he referred to as "Mackerel Reform".

I pried no further; I need my sleep.

Christopher had mistaken me for an agent of the Slobodov brothers when I came to the tavern using hand signals which he had misidentified as a coded introduction and had instantly approached me before Sedgewick, also an industrial spy, but for a rival South American group of Industrial Saboteurs, could step in and incapacitate me with the poisonous concoction that was coated onto his pet Ocelot claws for such an eventuality.

Manning paid the invoice he had obtained from the owner of the establishment, who thanked us for our custom and we departed for the Mutare Railway Station for the 160 mile journey.

During the first part of that journey, my compatriot explain the method he would employ to obtain the information he needed. It involved an elaborate computer program contained on something that he called an "Universal Serial Bus Stick" which had been hidden inside a plastic courgette as to avoid detection, a few other items were deployed within several other fake vegetables and fruit all provided by the brothers William and Benjamin to ease the purloining.

During a twenty minute "courtesy break" at Rusape Station, Manning, at my suggestion, bought a basket to place his various instruments of deception in as to make a more conducive appearance as it was his intension to don a white laboratory coat and walk straight through the front door of the Research Centre with the man he was meeting at the station; yet another victim of blackmail by the brothers Slobodov no doubt.

We then proceeded to Marondera. Christopher informed me that we would need an alternative mode of transport to Harare from there as the length of time it would take to access and attain the items of interest would mean that the train would have left. I assured him that I could, if necessary, purloin a car from the Research Centre car park utilising a trick taught to me during my incarceration by "Nobby" Clientelle, the notorious car heister of Monrovia which utilised a coat hanger and several fragmented lengths of nylon stocking all held together with a mixture made from molasses, sparrow vomit and lemon juice. Manning suggested I look for the spare key up on the driver's side sun visor, which I agreed might be better, quicker and a lot cleaner.

We are now back on board the Harare Express bound for nefarious deeds in Marondera...

Day 205

After a delay of some seventeen hours due to a four ton truck having been securely duck taped to the train track by the Anti-Mugabe Action for Zimbabwean Emancipation (AMAZE) as a form of protest, we arrived in Marondera at three o'clock in the morning.

The contact that Manning was supposed to have met with had obviously given up on ever meeting us and was now, presumably, tucked up in bed somewhere, so my involvement became completely necessary when Christopher decided that now was the best time for the incursion into the Research Park concealed by the cover of darkness.

Armed with the basket of bogus fruit and vegetables and with Manning holding his rubber banana, we made for the perimeter fence. Reaching it undetected we crouched down as Christopher rooted through the basket and produced a plastic mango that cleverly concealed a pair of wire cutters with which he proceeded to cut a hole in the mesh for us to enter by. Having successfully entered the grounds of the establishment, we crept forward to an open window I had espied whilst this erstwhile entrance was being created. There Manning withdrew from the basket a facsimile of a large carrot-shaped periscope he used to check the room was clear, which he nodded silently that it was and we clambered in; still undetected.

We were met with a harrowing sight.

The room through which we had gained egress was the Laboratory where they kept the animals they had experimented upon. Rows and rows of cages were instantly apparent in dim light of smoke alarm LED's. The smell was one that was almost pleasant, not unlike a fruit cocktail, but had an underlying taint, rather like a zoo. A noise in the containment next to me made me glance at the contents only to see what looked like an African Grey Parrot to which an almond had been grafted onto its face to replace its beak, another cage contained a Macaque monkey whose back was covered in what appeared to be mushrooms, but, upon closer inspection, just turned out to be a nasty allergic reaction to the pineapple marmoset which was crammed in the cage with it. Others, like the Zebra with a bunch of grapes sticking out of one ear and a strawberry for a nose, were just too horrific to recount. This place was run by monsters!

Manning had obtained, by way of his artificial banana, the information that was required by the Slobodov brothers and we decided to leave immediately; it was then I came to the decision that these poor creature should at least have an attempt at freedom and began to unlock and fling open the doors of the cages as we ran toward the exit.

The cacophony of sound that this course of action awoke the guard. There was only one on duty, and he was in an adjoining room and he would have apprehended us if it was not for the unfortunate guards forehead coming into contact with the coconut which had been riveted onto the left foot of a flamingo which was taking flight at that very moment.

Outside I ran toward a Land Rover Discovery which was parked near the wide open main gate, leapt into it and found the key already in the ignition. I started the engine and Manning jumped into the passenger seat just as the Monstrously Reformed Menagerie stampeded past us and onto freedom.

Our journey toward Harare was conducted in shocked silence...

Day 207

We have had to delay our arrival in Harare by taking a detour to Kariba Airport on the north coast of Lake Kariba to meet with the Slobodov brothers.

Christopher received the instructions on his mobile phone which was artfully concealed within a facsimile of an aubergine. The diversion meant that we overshot the capital by some 240 miles to journey to the west of Zimbabwe and close to the border of Zambia which runs, I am told, through the centre of the lake.

We arrived at the airport in the heat of the mid-afternoon when it appeared that everyone, except the two us and a few rabid dogs, had taken shelter against the heat; we pulled into one of the two hangers on the edge of the seas Manning had been instructed to do in his phone message. They were not difficult to find as they were the only structures at the airport aside from the control tower and a round fuel tank set dangerously close, it seemed to me, to the single runway. We decided to catch a few moments sleep whilst awaiting further instructions.

We were awoken by the snarling of one of the rabid dogs that had clambered onto the bonnet of the Land Rover and was chewing on the spare wheel which was affixed to it in addition to the one on the rear door. As we sat there wondering what to do the phone rang; I answered it as Manning tried to distract the dog with a bunch of synthetic radishes, it was William Slobodov with instructions for the delivery of the information.

A light aircraft would land shortly to take us north to Lusaka International Airport where a private jet was awaiting to fly us to Mexico; he would not be drawn into giving away any further information other than issue threats against mine and Christopher's families, he then hung up.

The dog had, during my stunted conversation, had run away yelping, the result of, I thought, of Manning brutish application of the radishes, but, as he informed me was actually caused by the discovery of the pineapple marmoset who had stowed away in the rim of the spare tyre. This little creature, it would appear, was an irritant to all other creatures apart from Homo sapiens, as Christopher was now cradling it in his hands with no adverse effect.

We met the aircraft with no problems and embarked upon the 9000 mile journey to Mexico almost immediately as we had only to walk three hundred yards across the concourse to the awaiting Cessna Citation Jet. I say almost no delay, Christopher insisted that he pack all his fake vegetables and fruit as they had "stood us in good stead so far".

I just cannot help thinking I am destined to do nothing but get transported around the globe to anywhere and everywhere except where I wish to go....

Day 208

Half way across the Atlantic on our way to Mexico on the Brothers' Slobodov's private executive jet Christopher, who appeared to have been well acquainted with the drinks cabinet since take off, made a confession to me in whispered, drunken tones.

He was not an author, as we had established a few days before, but neither was he just a victim of the Russian Mafia; he was in fact, he slurred confidentially, an agent for the very secret DI 25 (Department of Intelligence) and had been charged with the mission to disrupt or destroy the Slobodov's latest attack upon an unsuspecting world.

Nayarit, one of Mexico's 31 states, is located along the Pacific Ocean having its southern border with the state of Jalisco. This entire area is surrounded by mango orchards where approximately 1.5 million metric tons of mangoes are grown annually, making Mexico the third largest producer of mangoes after India and China; and most of it owned by the Slobodov brothers. The information that we had been carrying from the Research Centre was the blueprint for a virus which could devastate the world's production of the mango, along with a resistant strain to make other mangoes, namely William and Benjamin's, immune. Thus creating a world shortage of the most popular fruit on the planet, for which they would be the only providers.

Christopher looked carefully around once more and then proceeded forward to the aircrew cabin where, unlike commercial airlines, the door to the cockpit was unlocked. With him he carried a bunch of raspberries and the pineapple marmoset, which he told me were a security contingency and only for protection. He opened the door and with a wink in my direction leapt into the cabin and slammed the door shut behind him.

It was at this time I thought it prudent to strap myself in with the safety belt, and wondered where the parachutes were stored.

The aircraft lurched twice then started a steady bank to port. A familiar voice came over the intercom informing me that the flight plan had been changed and that the destination was now Sarasota International Airport, Florida. Christopher reappeared several moments later and left the door of the cabin open he placed the pineapple marmoset, who was now asleep, in the doorway.

He explained that after a brief struggle with the co-pilot, which accounted for the lurch, he had threatened the aircrew with our little friend the marmoset, who, he told me, had the ability to spray a liquid based on concentrated pineapple juice with high accuracy from a gland just at the back of the throat. It could be enticed to do so by flicking its left ear, and pacified by stroking the right one. What a little convoluted geneticized wonder!

Manning explained that we had been under observation by the co-pilot via closed circuit cameras so had have feigned inebriation as to fool him. I remarked that he had succeeded in fooling me also and he replied that it had taken years of research and practice to attain such a level of subterfuge. It made me feel immensely proud that our country is being protected by such dedicated professionals who were even prepared to overindulge in alcohol and build up their immunity just to ensure the security of the nation!

We celebrated with a gin and tonic or two.

I was well into the seventh shot of my immunity programme when the pilot called urgently from the cabin, though not so loud as to wake up the easily provoked pineapple marmoset. There was, apparently, bad weather between us and Florida. Hurricane Eric was to make landfall around Fort Lauderdale in the next hour, just as we would be approaching the peninsular. The pilot suggested diverting and, after a hurried radio message between Christopher and flight control we diverted to Guantanamo Bay, the American enclave in Cuba.

Here we go again.....

Day 209

The saying "the best laid plans of mice and men" does not cater for unforeseen incidents involving pineapple marmosets.

Just before entering the final approach to land at Guantanamo Bay the little creature awoke in a panic. Not knowing where it was and in unfamiliar surroundings, it bolted into the cockpit where, in its frantic attempts to escape whatever danger it had perceived, leapt onto the captains face, knocking his headphones askew, and proceeded to evacuate its poison gland up his left nostril. The crazed and terrorised miniature monkey then jumped to the co-pilot and started to chew off his earlobe.

Christopher cried out for me to assist him in removing both aircrew from the cockpit and restraining the genetically homogenised primate by trying to stroke its right ear as previously instructed. We administered first aid to the aircrew and sedated the genetically spliced simian by stapling it to a synthesized palm tree frond that Manning had been using to line the fruit basket and lightly beating it senseless with a toffee hammer.

On returning to the cockpit, we discovered that the auto-pilot had re-programmed itself and was now heading toward Jose Marti International Airport in Havana. Christopher did not think we would have any problems there as we are British and looked forward to purchasing some decent cigars as he only had two left, this reminded him of something and he left the cockpit. During the short flight to the capital of Cuba, Manning had taken the USB sticks from both the banana and courgette and placed them inside the cigars he had mentioned.

As I sat and waited in the seat vacated by the aurally incapacitated co-pilot, I noticed the date and realised that, if it had not have been for that tragic accident with a ride-on lawnmower and four itinerant beagles it would have been my mother's eighty-fourth birthday.

The plane started its decent, so did I into a depression that I had not suffered for many years; not since the unfortunate incident with the sweet trolley, a length of fire hose and Lady Newton-Fizz during the Debutants Ball at the Hilton Hotel which saw me served a lifetime ban from that renowned establishment.

Day 210

I write this relaxing on a terrace of a CIA safe house in the town of Santa Fe just west of Havana, watching the boats as they drift in and out of Marina Hemmingway sipping my first gin and tonic of the afternoon with the ever-present smell of Cuban cigars pervading the air.

Both Christopher and I are guests of the Central Intelligence Agency, who have had a clandestine presence on the island since the end of the Castro/Guevara revolution in 1959 when they ousted Batista, under the cover of posing as the "Cigar Import Advisory", which says a lot for the imagination of our American cousins and their Intelligence Services. They explain it away as saving money on the stationary.

We had landed safely at Jose Marti International Airport with no problems thanks to the Auto-Pilot, there we were met by a "Salesman" and flown the short distance to Santa Fe by helicopter. We had a pleasant evening and I relished a long hot soak in the bath, the first for a long time.

Now I while away my time writing this whilst waiting for Christopher to finish the debriefing with the CIA, our little pineapple marmoset, whom I have named "Marty", has calmed down completely since his 'episode' on the jet and now sits on my shoulder sedately eating grapes as I write to you. I do not know why animals seem to take to me so easily. Maybe I inherited the skill from my Great Grandfather, let's face it; he hunted enough of them, some to the point of extinction.

My musings were interrupted by the return of Manning with the CIA's most senior 'salesman' Geoffrey Cummings-Hardly, who, it transpired, was a relative of the Grand Dame Alicia Cummings-Hardly of Dumfriesshire whom my family was also distantly related.

Geoffrey had been seconded from MI6 by the CIA as they needed operatives who had a natural sounding non-American accent as the United States were not allowed to operate within the boundaries of the

Republic of Cuba, apart from the holiday home for retired terrorists in the enclave of Guantanamo Bay. He told me that, as he still had contacts within MI6, obtaining my papers (Passport travel and inoculation documents for Marty etc.), would be no problem at all, however, and whilst we were waiting for the necessary, there was a little job I could perform for them by way of payment.

They needed somebody to fly to Mexico to deliver what was now a rewritten version of the "Mango Virus" to the Brothers Slobodov.

My cover story was that the Jet had been struck by lightning as we clipped the tail end of Hurricane Eric and had diverted to Antigua for repairs; the flight records had been altered to back up this subterfuge. Manning, I would tell them, had suffered horrible disfigurement in the accident and would probably never play the harpsichord again. The original aircrew were willing to continue their journey as they had been promised American citizenship on completion of the mission and they hated the Slobodov's as both pilot and co-pilot had suffered horrendous torture by the brothers.

Apparently this is how they exert their dominance over people, and their methods appear horrific; the recounting of how they employed three toothpicks, a milk jug and a pneumatic drill to coerce a foreign diplomat into revealing sensitive information into the habits of the Bengalese Attaché to the United Nations will stay in my nightmares for a long while.

But I need those papers to return to you, my love, so it is into the jaws of death I must journey once more. Besides, the $350,000 US reward that I have been offered will not go amiss either.

Day 211

The day could have gotten off to a better start.

On arrival at the Slobodov Ranch I walked in on William pleasuring himself over pictures of oddly shaped vegetables on the internet. I apologised and left the room immediately, a few moment a dishevelled William Slobodov followed. Thankfully he did not decide to decapitate me with his small fruit dicer he always carried with him, but instead he acted like I had him at a disadvantage; which I did.

Ensuring him it would go no further (unless it benefitted me when the opportunity arose), I presented the computer stick which had been secreted in a cedar box containing 25 loose, Montecristo No 4, Cuban cigars. Then we walked amiably to the large terrace which overlooked the huge vividly green and perfectly manicured lawns of the Hacienda del Fruto Grande, where he ordered coffee from a very obviously nervous and subservient boy dressed in all white. Before the coffee arrived we were joined by William's brother, Benjamin and it was then I realised that they were identical twins! The only possible to tell them apart was the fact that William had black hair and Benjamin sport the same but with a brilliant white streak running through it on the left side, but had they both been wearing full-face ski masks, not even their own mother could have told them apart.

I introduced myself to the second Slobodov Brother who nodded by way of acknowledgement and sat in the vacant chair next to his brother. The subservient boy returned with a pot of hot coffee and three cups on a tray, but as he came closer to the brothers his nervousness got worse and he started to shake which became more and more pronounced as he approached us. It was obvious to me that he was petrified of the twins and to ensure he did not pass them with the tray he came around to my left, but as he drew level with me he noticed a glance from William and his trembling became so bad that he dropped the tray and the coffee spilled all over my white espadrilles but as I stood in surprised shock I managed to kick them off before the scalding liquid could penetrate to my feet.

William made sure I was shown to a nearby bathroom where I could run cold water on my feet, the manservant that appear was rather a bit more robust than the coffee boy and he brought with him some open-toed leather sandals for me to wear. He then showed me by way of pointing (with the middle finger of his right hand, as his index finger was missing) the way to the bathroom where he left me at the door to carry out my ministrations.

As I did not require any self-administered first aid, I decided to carry out a little clandestine reconnoitring of the Hacienda. I returned to a room where I had noticed the door slightly ajar and entered quietly. The room was a huge affair with white painted walls and cedar wood rafters set in a high ceiling and terracotta tiles on the floor. It was packed full of curious furniture and ornaments. A large sofa large enough for at least seven people commanded the centre of the room in front of a fire place so large it seemed like a room itself. Upon the arms of the sofa were delicately crocheted antimacassars which looked like pigmy Hippopotamus, and next to the right arm, perversely, was the stuffed skin of a pigmy hippopotamus carved to look like an antimacassar.

An assortment of vicious weapons and instruments of torture adorned the walls but there was a space in the centre of the far wall where there should have been something, but it had been taken down and I shuddered to think what it was. As I let my mind wander hideously as to what, or who, it could be utilised for I heard a scream from the veranda and I rushed toward the door in case I was discovered. I re-joined the Slobodov's just in time to see Benjamin dragging an utterly distraught coffee boy toward a large stables and I thought it prudent not to enquire as to his well-being, nor if the instrument missing from the large room was accompanying him.

I made a big show of checking my watch and telling William that I had to make my flight back to Cuba. I enquired whether there was a message for me to take back with me and he handed me a large bag which contained what appeared to be a dead chinchilla that had been shaved across the back and on which a message in Cyrillic characters had been tattooed, he apologised for the demise of the rodent, but, he went on to explain to would be far more prudent than having a live chinchilla rush about the aircraft and when I recalled the mayhem that dear little Marty caused I was inclined to agree; and my coffee stained espadrilles.

I bid him well and left post haste to be driven in their Bentley Continental Spur to the airfield just outside Puerto Valarta where the jet was waiting, I cannot how express how relieved I felt to be leaving behind those devilish twins......

Day 213

The plight of the servants at Hacienda del Fruto Grande and the torture they suffer at the hands of the sadistic Slobodov Brothers has been weighing heavily on my mind. As I sat on my veranda last night stroking Marty and listening to that most traditional of Cuban music; the acapella version of the BeeGees Greatest Hits which was wafting over the bay from a Taverna, I decided to have words with Geoffrey Cummings-Hardly about taking action against the Russian twins.

I spoke to him on the telephone and he very quickly agreed, to my mind, a bit too eagerly; especially when I mentioned the room with the torture equipment.

A course of action was decided upon that evening between Manning, Cummings-Hardly and myself. We would pay a visit to Mexico the very next day under the pretence of selling the Slobodov Brothers more industrial secrets from the Research Centre in Africa. They agreed enthusiastically and we commissioned the Jet once more and left early this morning. During the flight, Geoffrey quizzed me most intensely about the kind of instruments of torture contained in that room and paid particular (if not unhealthy to my mind) interest when I mentioned the Iron Lady I had espied.

Once at the Hacienda we sat on the same veranda that I had witnessed the ordeal of the coffee boy, whom was nowhere to be seen, I might add. Christopher produce reams of paper from a briefcase which he proclaimed to be figures and blueprint which would revolutionise the production of mangoes. He also presented them with another box of Cuban Cigars which he told the brothers conspiratorially were actually meant for Fidel Castro himself and had been liberated from the Interior Ministry. The Brothers, being Russian immediately fell upon the cigars and helped themselves to one each. Manning provided the lighter and William and Benjamin settled down to enjoy the finest tobacco that the Caribbean could produce.

After a few moments, I could not help but notice that they both had turned a slight shade of green, then their faces proceeded to range through most of the colours of the rainbow. With a cry of "Сволочи!" (Bastards) William stood up and clutched his neck and slumped over his brother who twitched once and then sat still; The Brothers Slobodov were no more!

To say I suffered a shock and panic at their sudden demise would be an understatement, especially as I had partaken of a gin and tonic as had they and I was convince that was the cause of their sudden and painful passing. But my panic was assuaged by Geoffrey explaining that it was the cigars, not the drink that were poisoned. They had indeed been cigars destined for the Cuban Revolutionary Leader but in 1962 and had been laced with arsenic by the CIA, but they had never been used.

That was all the explanation that I received from Geoffrey as then he insisted that I show him "The Room". As we approached the Hacienda he was almost salivating at the thought of the Instruments of suffering that awaited. Christopher started to organise the servants to dispose of the corpses, a job that they all seemed very willing to perform.

I wish I could explain my trepidation as we approached the room that was the sole interest of my companion of espionage, his enthusiasm was most distasteful and once we had reached the door he dismissed me in a very offhanded manner and entered the room bolting the door behind him.

I decided to return to the veranda and proceed with my "Gin and Tonic Immunity Programme" which I did with nearly the same gusto as Cummings-Hardly had shown for the Torture Room. I was well into my eighth phase of my invulnerability training when Manning returned and enquired as to the location of Geoffrey. I slurred to him I had not seen him for over two hours ago when he locked himself into the room. Christopher requested that I show him where the Room was and I stood, somewhat unsteadily, to make our way back to the Hacienda. As we approached I was remarking that the lemons seemed to be a lot stronger in Mexico as I could not walk in a straight line, when a loud crash was heard from the aforementioned room.

We ran to the source of the sound only to find that the door was still locked, Christopher picked up a large brass candlestick holder and proceeded to batter the door open with loud encouragement from me.

The scene that greeted us when egress had been achieved was not a pretty one.

Cummings-Hardy must have been stood on the top of a bookcase trying to reach one of the many implements of torment upon the walls when the bookcase had tipped over and propelled the unfortunate agent into the Iron Lady that he had seemed so unhealthily interested in before. The large cast iron spikes within the casket had penetrated his torso in several places and his body still twitched slightly as we rushed to his aid. It was obvious to both Christopher and myself that no amount of aid would save our ill-fated companion and as we looked on he passed away.

It is a scene that only, I hope, time will erase.

But I am convince that I will go to my own grave still seeing the ecstatic smile upon Cummings-Hardly's face and, clutched tightly in his hand the utensil of pain that he had lost his life to procure – the dreaded musical triangle!

Day 215

I say farewell to Cuba today with, I must admit, some sadness, after all my travels to date, I find it the most pleasant and welcoming place I have seen so far. I also say goodbye to my friend Christopher Manning who has been requested to replace the most luckless Geoffrey Cummings-Hardly and he had accepted the position with a healthy salary increase.

I have to leave as we have received information from the Hacienda del Fruta that the man Sedgewick, and his poison clad Ocelot Simon are on my trail and has vowed to never return to Mexico until I am dead; a revenge killing for causing the demise of his employers, which ended the most lucrative period of his employed life as a spy and hitman for the Brothers Slobodov.

Another element which necessitated my prompt departure from that Caribbean Isle was the news that the long-time girlfriend of William Slobodov is also on the trail for revenge; none other than Bessie McTavish!

So I found myself, once more, ensconced on board a boat which is used to secretly ferry Cuban Cigars to the States (and the smell seeps through the loose fitting hold doors) and setting sail across the Gulf of Mexico to Naples in Florida.

Naples is situated north of the Everglades and consists mainly of yachting harbours, holiday homes and golf courses, one of which I found myself overlooking from a CIA sponsored safe house on Banyan Boulevard. They assured me that it was indeed secure and the only perceived threat was that of alligators, but as Marty the pineapple marmoset was with me, they should be no problem. The catering was all taken care of by a chef who lived in the house next door and provided the meals freshly cooked. So, as I found myself tucking into a T bone steak, done to perfection, and Marty was dining on a mixture of nuts and vegetation, a note was brought to my attention.

No so much the note, but the medium sized rock it was attached to, as it smashed through the large glass patio door and landed on the dining table in front of me deeply scratching the fine mahogany veneer. I opened the note with some trepidation and read it.

"Bargain Double Glazing available NOW!" It read, "Patio Doors a Speciality!" in small letters underneath the advert it informed "Veneer Repairs Available at Cheeeeep Rates!" I made a note of the number.

Day 220

It was my birthday three days ago, which means I'm younger than my fingernails but older than my teeth!

In a fit of depression that only the realisation of your own mortality can bring as you notice that everything is heading south at a rate of knots; I decided to go out and continued my "Gin Resistance" exercises.

I remember going into a Jazz-Funk-Classical Clarinet-Brass Band and Heavy Metal Crossover Bar called "Noise" and meeting some seemingly nice people, I do not recall their names; but there was rather a lot of them and I also recall listening with great intent to a Thrash Metal interpretation of Queen's "Somebody to Love" and accompanying it with a vuvuzela before falling off the stage and into a large fish bowl full of, what appeared to me, to be cough supplements.

I now find myself in Paris with no idea of how I got here, who I travelled with, nor what I can do to return as my poor pineapple marmoset Marty is still in Florida. It would be a simple matter, given my recent experiences, for me to cross over to dear England and you, my love, but I feel I owe my little genetically interfered friend loyalty as he has helped me a great deal.

It is with this in mind that I must find the American Consulate and see what my friends at the "Cigar Import Advisory" are able to do for me.

Day 223

Have spent the last few days waiting for information about Marty the pineapple marmoset and when I can travel to get him. The American Consulate are very accommodating since they received a call from Christopher in Cuba and, rather than my going to Florida, are flying my miniature primate pal directly from Fort Lauderdale International Airport in a crate especially designed by the Cretin Brothers, to whom the rock and business flyer that came through the patio door in Naples belonged.

Due to the tight live animal import rules in France imposed due to the infamous Barkness Circus Incident which involved three lions, a clown and two juggling dwarves (I believe that Reigate may never recover from the experience); I will have to travel to Agadir in Morocco to collect Marty and, after disguising him as a novelty battery operated pepper grinder, attempt to smuggle him into Europe via Gibraltar.

I have, this moment, received the notification that I am travelling imminently to North West Africa to be reunited with my genetically confused miniature ape forthwith. I have to disguise myself as a fur coat and be encased within a large dark oak wardrobe (the Americans really do know how to travel) to circumnavigate the need for official documents; the logic being, if I haven't left the country legally how can I re-enter illegally? Not sure about that one.......

Day 225

My journey to Agadir was very sedate, arriving at Al Massira airport just in time for tea, to which I was guided by Daphne Alba, representative of the Cigar Import Advisory to Morocco, who, she took great lengths in informing me, was an "Expert in all matters British."

Over a cooling cup of Earl Grey, where she proved without doubt that she was not an Anglophile at all by putting milk in her tea, she told me that Marty's progress was slower than expected with an unscheduled stop after the flight diverted to Gibraltar and the pineapple marmosets escort, Chuck Normal, had release him from his specially designed crate built by then same people that had thrown their advertising through my patio door, and Marty had then gotten himself mixed into a troupe of Barbary apes and it had taken several hours for Chuck to find him again.

Showing what was, for an American agent, a modicum of intelligence, Normal utilised a combination of a bag of Marty's favourite nuts, an electronic cattle prod and a pistol firing tranquilizer darts. Thankfully he had only sedated and shocked his way through seventy percent of the primate population of the British Enclave before he found Marty and made his escape from the angry mob of animal rights protesters who were there on a convention and were gathered for a 'team photo' with the apes.

Alba assured me that my friend would be arriving at this very airport in around an hour on a privately chartered plane; but worryingly, she also told me that there is a "package" from Christopher Manning and it is marked "For Your Eyes Only" which fills me with dread: what if it is the DVD of Roger Moore's worst performance as James Bond?

Day 227

The strange package arrived with Marty my pineapple marmoset, but remained unopened for well over two hours as my little genetically variegated primate pal was so pleased to see me that he monopolised my attention entirely, even to the total exclusion of Daphne and Chuck. But, as they seemed to be involved in a reunion of a more covertly carnal nature, they never seemed to notice. When my diminutive companion had finally calmed down, he settled onto my left shoulder and curled up and slept. This gave me the opportunity to open the "For Your Eyes Only" package.

Thankfully it was not the Roger Moore film, but, perhaps more worrying it contained a request from Manning in his capacity as the new Head of Operations of the Cigar Import Advisory in Cuba. He was requesting my aid in a clear up operation to obtain the remnants of the Brothers Slobodov's empire before Bessie McTavish could get her hands on it.

I misunderstood the location at first – Skive; I thought it was an invitation to do nothing, but it turns out it is a town in Northern Denmark on the shores of the Skive Fjord. I was to be flown to Karup Airport where it would be a short twenty-six mile drive (forty-two kilometres in foreignese, apparently). Bessie, and her new Beau Sedgewick, complete with his poison coated Ocelot, Simon, had been "detained" in Miami Airport under an egregious charge of gross breach of copyright when a bottle of pirated Channel No.5 had been found hidden not too well under the four kilo bags of cocaine in their luggage.

The mission was to find the storage facilities that the brothers had been using to stow nefarious objects along with items of a more dubious nature which they would have used to flood the European Market and undermine the Authorities.

So, once again, I find myself on board the Jet that we "borrowed" from the Slobodov Estate winging our way to Northern Europe; if you are awake at 2.30 am and you are looking out of your bedroom window toward the east and see a small flashing moving across the sky in a northerly direction; please give me a wave.

Day 229

The past two days have been a blur.

I arrived in Denmark safely enough, but the driver, a Frenchman called Robert Degass, had no idea where we were going (the mission was on a need to know basis, and apparently the Americans in their wisdom decided that the driver did not need to know, I surprised they did not blindfolded him.), and took me in the entirely wrong direction and, being as we had never been to Denmark before, it was not until we were in the outskirts of Aalborg that we realised. The SatNav should have helped, but it had been programmed with an old map of Yugoslavia and the voice, in Erdu, was directing us to a whorehouse in Podgorica, Montenegro.

Needless to say, Bessie MacTavish and Sedgewick got to the warehouse in Skive before we did and were lying in wait when I finally arrived. Simon the Ocelot had been purged of the poison coating his claws and it had been replaced with a quick acting sedative. The wild cat might have missed me had it not been for Robert stepping on him as we entered the darkened storage facility, and with a wail like a Banshee the furious feline scratched my lower legs and I almost instantly sank into the arms of Morpheus.

When I regained what passes for consciousness these days, I was bound and gagged in the hold of a boat heading I knew not. Luckily both MacTavish and Sedgewick had missed Marty who had been asleep in the specially design inside pocket of my jacket and he was able to untie me (a trick that Chuck had taught him, thankfully, on the flight from Florida) whilst I planned our escape. I did not know how long I had been unconscious, but it was dark when I gained covert access to the deck of the boat, a four berth yacht which was registered in Portsmouth and was steadily cruising in, if my star gazing was correct, a southerly direction.

The noise of my egress was disguised somewhat by the painful squeals of Degass emanating from the main bunk; he was obviously being subjected to Bessie's particular bent of ministrations. The awful image of Santiago, the prison guard suffering at the hands of Ms MacTavish sent a shudder through me and I had a sudden pang of sympathy for Robert, despite him being French.

I was crawling around a bulkhead toward the bridge when I came face to face with Sedgwick and Simon the ocelot, luckily they had not seen me yet so my attack was swift and unexpected. The brief battle between myself and Sedgewick was not a pretty one and my use of a boathook, a piece of the ensign from the flagpole and the edge of a discarded paper plate was somewhat gratuitous, but effective. And Marty had overcome Simon with his ability of being highly infectious to other animals, so we bound them together and placed them both in the lifeboat and set them adrift on the North Sea.

Bessie was a lot harder to dispatch, not only due to her enormous bulk which made it very difficult to eject her from the forward berth, but also that she had riveted Robert between her breasts and navel and the risk of asphyxia to the poor Gallic male was an ever present threat. But in the end dear old Marty came through once more and sprayed her several times with his citric ejections until she submitted and I was able to crowbar the unfortunate Frenchman from her body with only a few marks and a very nasty gash to his torso which should heal in a year or two.

As she had wedged herself into the forward bunk so effectively I had to leave Bessie were she was, and as she had slipped into unconsciousness after the unceasing salival attack of my miniature primate, I considered her not to be a risk.

The main risk, as I discovered upon my entering the bridge was the oilrig that the boat was approaching at a high rate of knots. But with the minimal amount of rushing about and randomly pushing buttons and pulling levers I was able to slow our approach to a crawl which enabled us to hurl the injured Frenchman onto a platform at sea level at the foot of one of the metallic leviathan's legs and myself and Marty joining him immediately. We stood shivering on the meshed podium inches from the surface of the icy North sea and watched as the motor yacht slowly motored away into the murk carrying Bessie away for, hopefully, good. But we shall see.

I now write this sitting in a bunk on the rig with Marty curled up asleep on my lap and Robert Degass sleeps peacefully in a drug induced coma in the medical centre. I am assured by the rig manager, Bertram Echoecho, a Swedish count apparently, that there will be a schedule flight of a helicopter in a few days which will take me to Aberdeen.

I cannot wait!!

Day 234

The helicopter had been delayed for 26 hours due to inclement weather and a forty foot swell on the North Sea but it arrived safely yesterday morning. I helped with the disembarkation of the only passenger and when he was divulged of his total immersion suit and flying helmet I had a shock; it was my old friend Christopher Manning!

It seemed the world was about to fall apart once more and only me and my little monkey mate could save it, I was on the point of refusing when Manning dropped the bombshell; I was now a full agent for the Cigar Import Advisory with a salary commensurate with my position and a nice shiny badge (with a smaller one for Marty), which, due to the covert nature of the job, I could not show to anybody.

My mission was a difficult and dangerous one.

The warehouse in Skive was empty and it was thought that all the contents had been stowed on the motor cruiser that I had left MacTavish on. The boat had run aground on the beach at Scarborough and she had absconded with whatever the cargo had been but had been spotted chartering a small cargo plane from a private airfield nearby and, if the flight plan was to be believed, was heading to an ex-RAF station in Germany.

Manning thought that due to my history with the demented woman, I would jump at the chance to "remove her from society". He was right, not only because of what she had done, but what she could do in the future; I could never return home and relax with her at large (literally, given her size).

Once I had agreed, Christopher passed me a suitcase containing my instructions and various pieces of equipment that he thought I may need to aid my capture or otherwise of that evil woman. I could review these and my directives on the helicopter which was fuelled and ready to take me to Gutersloh.

Once we were in the air I opened the case to see what delights it held. It was full of items which would back up my cover as an international toy salesman

I found a rubber pen, which, if you turned the top in an anti-clockwise direction, became a pencil; a novelty "Grotto the Clown" watch that was, according to its brochure impervious to the electro-magnetic pulse of a nuclear explosion and automatically adjusted the time to whatever time zone you were in but nowhere were in the instructions did it tell me how to wind it up and the arms of Grotto were permanently stuck at 10.17. Amongst the plethora of small items the case also contained a small figure of one of the villains of the Star Wars series which held several USB ports secreted over several parts of its body and could be used to wirelessly connect to any computer system with twelve feet and could be used to covertly download files. The one item of equipment which was sadly missing was a weapon and as my edict was to "Capture, detain or eliminate" MacTavish one would be quite useful, I would have to improvise.

As I was filling out the simple 184 page questionnaire and personal details as required for the position, I could not help notice a crate with ventilation holes standing in the furthest corner of the helicopter and, upon requesting information from the co-pilot, was informed that it was the pet Mallard, called Willard, of Bertram Echoecho who was being returned to Sweden to see a vet as his feathers were falling out and his bill was wilting.

I had reach page 178 "Name and Occupation of your Great Great Uncle and his inside leg measurements" in the section entitled "Intensely Personal, but Pointless Questions part 2b section four (all questions require answers)" and was filling in the "Any Further Information" box , when Marty awoke and jumped from his perch to investigate the crate containing Willard the Mallard. The duck emitted a high pitched "Quack!" as he broke out with an intense allergic reaction to the proximity of my pineapple marmoset and proceeded to thrash around the crate, breaking free and attempting to take flight to escape the irritation caused by Marty. He flashed past me and straight into the cabin where he began to lash about breaking instruments and the nose of the pilot, the co-pilot had already been incapacitated when the duck had flown into the back of his head forcing him into the windscreen.

The helicopter began to plummet toward the ground at a high rate of knots, but with only feet to spare the pilot regained control enough to bring it to a very bumpy landing. Before he lost consciousness he informed me that we were somewhere near Antwerp in Belgium, and my Satellite Navigation system disguised as a colander confirmed this. I then utilised my "emergency mobile communication device" which look very much like a cuddly pink hippopotamus to contact the Belgian Emergency Services. I managed to gather up Marty and Willard the Mallard who had been dazed by the crash landing, placing the duck into my briefcase.

I then thought it most opportune, once I had checked that the aircrew were still breathing, if I beat a hasty retreat into a nearby copse of trees to avoid any awkward questioning by the incumbent Officers of the Law who would be attending the site.

Once in the trees I activated my squeaking plastic blue frog, which was actually an emergency beacon, which broadcast a high frequency croak from my location, through GCHQ and directly to Manning's office then I sat back and awaited rescue.

I looked at my watch; it was 10.17

Day 236

I was left lying in the copse of trees awaiting contact from Manning for several hours. My time was taken up by keeping Marty, my pineapple marmoset, and Willard the Mallard separated and watching the Belgian Emergency Services trying to pry the aircrew out of the mangled helicopter with the aid of a surgical truss, two syringes and a stretcher from an ambulance. An ambulance which was later hijacked by five roaming Somalian refugees and used to attempt entry into the UK by posing as a bipartisan freelance medical specimen jar juggling troupe.

My contact arrived at around 3 in the afternoon, I nearly did not notice her as she had disguised herself as a small electrical pylon and had been slowly edging toward my clump of foliage most of the day to avoid detection, but she was hyper-allergic to duck down and even the small amount of plumage that had managed to cling to Willard had been enough to irritate her nasal passages, and the strange sight of an angular metal construction convulsing in a sneezing fit was a strange one to behold. Luckily the Belgian Emergency Services did not see her as they were fighting off a gang of Romanians who were attempting to commandeer the water bowser accompanying the fire engine and utilise it as a means of transport to Zeebruge where most of them would conceal themselves in the water tank and, presumably, tread water whilst the ferry "Viking Nightnurse" navigated across the North Sea toward Felixstowe.

My contact, Miss Evaline Bohemia-Evans was from the distaff side of the Welsh wing of the Bohemia-Evans' who infamously caused a minor fracas at the 1844 third ashes test at Lords by ordering coffee instead of the traditional tea at four O'clock; an ignominious course of action that will forever overshadow that noble lineage (Even the fourth Earl of Gwent was refused entry in the House of Lords for three weeks because his man servant once served at the Bohemia-Evans' summer residence in Prestatyn).

My new instructions, according to Eva Evans, were to proceed to accompany her to Liege by means of bicycles, where we would then proceed to Aachen by Sinclair C5 where we would change transport once again as to not raise suspicion. But as the batteries on the tandem invalid carriage we would collect there only had a range of 20 kilometres we would have to abandon them at Eschweiler where we would board a train to Wuppertal and then on to Gutersloh by moped which we are now awaiting the delivery of...

Day 238

Our journey across Belgium and the German border was relatively straight forward aside from an unscheduled stop at Welkenraedt as the Logistics department had failed to fully connect the recharge lead to the battery of Eva Evans' C5 and every time she pedalled she received a minor electric shock.

Whilst we were awaiting the repairs, I took her to a bierkeller where I had noticed a poster advertising a Neo-Nazi rally. Imagine my shock and horror when I realized that it was not, as I had thought, a group of right-wing aficionados of the Matrix Trilogy but a gathering for some of life's more esoteric and radical thinking psychopaths. I was just about to apologise to Eva when the doors of the establishment were thrown open and several canisters of tear gas and two "flash bangs" hurled into the bar and armed personnel clad in black smashed through the windows; then all hell broke loose.

I managed to manhandle Eva out of the keller by flashing my secret insignia at the figure guarding the now shattered front door, I realise I should not show my badge, but needs must as they say. The raid, it transpired, was by a faction of the Israeli Special Forces; Mossad. So when they realised I worked ostensibly for the Americans, both Eva and I were released into the care of the local representative of the Computer Interactive Association (Belgium) Branch.

We collected our C5's from the garage and proceeded, in slow and somewhat shocked silence toward Aachen. Once there we transferred to the tandem invalid carrier with no problems at all; there was even a very handy wire basket in which to place my case of secret novelty items and the crate holding Willard! The train journey was relaxing and we slept most of the way before disembarking in Gutersloh.

As we stood at the large entrance of the Bahnhof Eva informed me that there had been an update from Manning and the Storage facility we were looking for was not actually, as previously thought, on the old

RAF Station, but in a village just outside it called Harsewinkel; I must admit that at this time I was beginning to wonder if all of this was a rather over-elaborate joke at my expense.

Day 240

The storage facilities in Harsewinkel was large, but almost completely devoid of its expected bounty.

I say almost because there were a few papers blowing about as we opened the door and Eva discovered a small yellow toad which had been genetically spliced with a lemon sitting in an old dog bowl of water, his skin exuding a concentrate of juice. As we searched for further evidence I could not help but notice the sound of barking emanating from behind another door at the rear of the facility.

I cautioned Eva that I was going to open it and I crept forward. No sooner had I opened the door I was forced into the wall as a tidal wave of dogs of all kind of breeds spilled through and filled the room; there must have been at least a hundred of them! They conducted a frantic canine smelling-spree by rushing around the room with their noses to the floor for several minutes whilst Eva and I just stood still as a precaution; but there was no sense of danger from them, they all seemed to be so happy at being set free and ignored us mainly. Then as one, they all made a bolt for the door in a barking mass; the more agile leading the way and they all disappeared through it, with a small Bichon Frieze and a Dachshund bringing up the rear.

As the dust settled in the subsequent silence, Eva showed me one of the sheets of paper that had been discovered on the floor before the canine intervention. It revealed that MacTavish and Sedgewick had obtained the research documents from Africa; the one she had handed me described a method for crossing the DNA of a snake with that of a pig (would that be a Snig or a Pake?) thus producing a porker that would regularly slough its skin which could undermine the entire pork scratching's industry in the UK!

I made the decision that, as Willard the Mallard had been entrusted to me, I would travel to Sweden and deliver him to Commander Echoecho's vet and Eva would take the documents to

Manning. She mulled this over carefully as, I had noticed, she tended to do with everything. Eva is a very intelligent girl, it's such a shame she's so damned ugly; she looks like the back end of the bus that Tina Turner ran into when it collided with Lionel Richie. She left me to catch a train to the Hook of Holland and me to Hamburg to meet the jet at the airport there.

It was also decided that, because of my apparent empathy with small creatures, I would take the lemon toad that she had christened Cedric, with me. I did not argue that point. The toads' skin needs to be kept moist and I have found that he relishes an afternoon bath in tonic water with an amount of gin added as an astringent. The trouble is, how do I dispose of a pint of it when he has finished his soak? It's a hard life when you are seconded to the service of protecting mankind.

As my train left the Bahnhof I could not help but notice a stream of seemingly wild dogs racing along one of the platforms, with a small Bichon Frieze and a Dachshund bringing up the rear.

Day 242

I spent most of yesterday in the Accidents and Emergency Department of Hamburg's Krankenhaus with a broken arm.

It's not mine, I found it on a park bench; but it is definitely broken.

The local Polizei are looking for the rest of the body it came from as I write; no sign of it yet but there are reports that a nostril has been found in Bremerhaven. I managed to sidestep the issue of whether or not I had perpetrated the monstrous act upon a fellow human being by introducing the Chief of Police, Karl Mainz, to Cedric's ablutions and after having to administer several rinsing's of my lemon toad, he saw that a man of my standing could never have had anything to do with the crime.

He also mention several dozen times that I was his newest "Beste Freunde" and clapped me on the right shoulder where I know I am going to have sustained deep bruising. A few times he hit me so hard that I had to restrain Marty from attacking him, it would not aid me one jot if my new acquaintance had been subdued by a concentrated pineapple-based acid attack; besides the toad expulsion combined with the gin were doing the job just fine.

It was then that a Police car dispatched to pick up the Chief arrived and I helped the nice officers pour the inebriated Chief Constable Mainz into the back of the vehicle with him singing 'Goodbye Lemon Tipped Toad', that not so well known Elton John song, in a high squeaky voice.

That, sadly, was the penultimate time anybody saw of Chief Constable Mainz. He commandeered the vehicle when the two constables stopped for a toilet break and he drove off, weaving down the Autobahn to Mohne where the last sighting of him was when he tried to hang glide from the top of the dam using a large handkerchief and his green Polizei issue jacket as a wind-brake. According to eyewitnesses he would have made it too had it not been for a sudden updraft taking him upward and into the trees to the north of the dam. His body has not been found.

The armless and mono-nostrilled body has been, however, and have been identified as the mortal remains of none other than Sedgewick. He must have fallen foul of Ms. MacTavish and she has disposed of his services in her own immutable way. There is no sign of Simon the poison ocelot who may well be wandering around the region pining for his master.

This has come as a great surprise and I have messaged Christopher Manning and he is this moment flying to see me to discuss our next course of action to take against MacTavish. So I will just have to bathe Cedric again.

Day 243

Christopher Manning arrived in the early hours of the morning and awoke me from my toad excretion induced slumber; note to self the G+T immunisation does not seem to be working, must try harder.

With over half of the Northern Polizei distracted with the search for Chief Constable Mainz, Manning decided that we would "obtain" the body of Sedgewick from the mortuary and take it back with us for closer examination by our own experts to see if there were any clues as to MacTavish's whereabouts.

When we arrived at the mortuary on Gutenabendhimmel Strasse there was only one guard on duty at the desk and he was so engrossed by the live feed at the search for the missing Chief that he did not even notice us when we passed the desk in and on the way out with the body bag. Given the normal ruthless efficiency of the German Polizei, I could not believe how easy it had been. The only hiccup had been the fact that Simon the Ocelot was in the morgue pining for his deceased owner, so much so that he had been easily overpowered, taking only four blows to the head with a hard copy of Grey's Anatomy to subdue him enough to place him inside the bag containing the mortal remains of Sedgewick.

The next problem was, due to the entire road system in the immediate area having been cordoned off (standard practice, apparently), the van was over seven hundred metres away, on Angelamerkell Strasse. We had to cut through Potsenjamsen Strasse and along Dontenrecallenbeindiswaybefore Strasse, but we were not seen at all; even when we passed a large Bierkeller full of off duty Polizei who were pre-emptually toasting the memory of their leader, whom, it would appear, was not going to be greatly missed, judging by the singing and cavorting that was spilling into Disisareallysillyandpointlesslylongnamefora Strasse.

The obligatory Black Van was just around the corner and we carefully placed the body bag into the back. There was a large wooden box containing various tools and items which we emptied and placed the comatose form of Simon, who, as I noticed as we placed the feline in its temporary secure containment, should be known as Simone.

Manning drove to a small private airfield where a light aircraft was waiting to take us to the UK. At last! I was returning to my native land!!

During the loading we received news that Chief Constable Mainz has been found. He was discovered in the woods surrounding the Mohne Lake hanging upside down suspended by the braces of his Lederhosen which he insisted on wearing under his uniform. He was softly singing "Lemon Bird high up in banana tree", an old calypso song and occasionally lapsing into quotes from Goethe.

Day 245

Yet another of my carefully thought out and meticulously planned escape has been thwarted.

As we were flying first to the UK with the remains of Sedgewick, I hatched a plot to leave Manning and the Cigar Import Advisory, or as it is known in Britain; Clowns In America, by way of utilising one of the many "Inflate-O-Mat®" expandable rubber novelty suits in my case. I though the Japanese Diplomat might suit my needs best (I had at first favoured the "Obese American Tourist", but it would have taken far too long to blow up).

It may have been the several bus and train timetables that I had printed from the Internet, or the fact that I kept whistling "If You Are Going to Abergavenny"; the site of my ancestral home, that gave Manning a hint of what I was plotting.

No matter how he pre-empted my daring escape, he managed to subdue me with a tincture of the sleeping draft coating on Simone the Ocelot's claws which he surreptitiously introduced into my third Gin and tonic of the flight and once more I plummeted into oblivion.

I awoke back in Cuba on a Chaise Lounge once owned, I believe, by the Marxist revolutionary Ernesto "Che" Guevara and a quote had been hastily embroidered upon the arm "Before the invasion, the revolution was weak. Now it's stronger than ever." A reference to the disastrous Bay of Pigs invasion by America in 1961.

I cannot describe the disappointment that I felt having missed the chance of even stepping foot on my beloved country, but Manning, who was sitting in a large chair behind a massive mahogany desk watching me, assured me that when my unconscious body was being moved to the executive jet my right arm fell from the stretcher and brushed the tarmac of Northolt Airport.

I shall not wash it for at least a week.

The examination of Sedgewick's body had yielded little by way of information leading to the discovery of Bessie's whereabouts, however his wallet, which had fallen out of an orifice that is best not described here during the placing of the corpse onto the examination table, contained detailed plans of the hideaway of MacTavish, including a plan of action, maps and timetables for bus and train, what a coincidence.

They indicated that MacTavish had fled and concealed self on a small Island, no bigger than 5 square kilometres, named Ostrov Matveyev, in the Pechora Sea of the northern coast of Russia and to the south of the Barents Sea. It was a haunt of the now deceased Slobodov Brothers and there was an underground complex where they hid most of their ill-gotten gains.

As it was mid-winter, the sea would be frozen solid and egress to the island could be achieved by something Manning referred to as a "Skidoo" which sounded rather like some kind of paddle game for children. But the noise may alert Bessie and we had no idea of any alarm system there may be set up at the frozen fortress. So, as time was of the essence, we were going to parachute onto the island to maintain the element of surprise.

I pointed out that the biggest flaw of that particular course of action was that I had never hurled myself out of a fully functional aircraft before, so Christopher signed me up for a crash course in parachuting; unfortunately the Ramon Balboa Skydiving School was fully booked for a week. A change of plan was called for, and Manning announced that the Salesperson who had delivered Marty to me in Europe would be accompanying us on the flight and that he would be living up to his name. He pressed a button on the desk and in walked Chuck Normal.

I elected to wait for the first available course at the Ramon Balboa Skydiving School.

Day 250

A cancellation at the Ramon Balboa Skydiving School meant I took the course a bit earlier than intended. I found that I quite enjoyed the exhilaration at rushing toward the ground; the only moment of doubt I had was on the first jump when I suddenly and irrationally wondered what would happen if I missed – if I just totally avoided the Earth and shot past it into space?

I think I have to give the gin a miss.

Because of the extremely low temperatures inside the Arctic Circle we will be leaving the ever-growing menagerie of Marty, Cedric and Simone (who has apparently succumbed to my empathic nature and actually purrs when she sees me) behind for their own wellbeing and I must admit to feeling rather vulnerable without them.

I am now flying with several members of a covert force (they would not tell me who they were but they did say it rhymes with Special Hair Service), in a C130 Hercules transport plane, (there are no identifiable markings on it, but they tell me it rhymes with 'naff'). I am dressed in the same snow camouflage uniform and parachute, but I am not qualified to carry a weapon, which to my way of thinking defeats the object of me being here really. I have, however, been able to hide about my person several items from my suitcase.

A novelty Inflate-O-Mat® four foot rabbit suit which in fact houses a pair of extendable electric skis, a novelty Inflate-O-Mat® bed of nails which is really a satellite radio transmitter, a novelty Inflate-O-Mat® play cooker which is essentially a robotic husky, a novelty Inflate-O-Mat® squeaky hammer which is actually a cleverly disguised real hammer and, finally a pea shooter; but with no peas.

I must give my suitcase full of inflatables a miss.

Manning has given me an update on Bessie MacTavish:

She has spent some of the huge fortune she has 'obtained' from the demise of the Brother's Slobodov and has undergone expensive extensive reconstructive surgery. It would appear that she has had a total body reformation akin to a Fay Weldon novel and her face has been completely repaired. She no longer looks like a character out of a tale by Victor Hugo, but more like Donnie Darko's mother, who it seems, overcome by the tragic loss of her son, got divorced, then married to the President of the USA, then died when aliens invaded Earth and then, in what could only be a bizarre twist of fate, was resurrected as President herself to battle aliens and defeat them.

I think I have to give the On Demand Movies a miss.

Day 251

Not many people, I suppose, know how hard snow is. When you think of it, it's stiff water and if you belly-flop into a swimming pool; it hurts.

So when travelling downward at about 140 miles per hour and your Inflate-O-Mat® bed of nails which is really a satellite radio transmitter, and the novelty Inflate-O-Mat® play cooker which is essentially a robotic husky, prematurely activate at eight thousand feet they do tend to increase your terminal velocity somewhat and my impact was slightly enhanced.

After two members of the Social Care Society had kindly dug me out of the five foot deep crater, we filled in the hole, which now contained the decimated radio and the extremely bent robotic husky to avoid detection, and I activated my Inflate-O-Mat® four foot rabbit extendable electric skis and we set off on our five mile trek over the frozen tundra toward the isle of Ostrov Matveyev and Bessie's secret hideout.

There were no real problems on the way, if I discount an over-amorous polar bear who mistook the rabbit for a mate and trying to copulate with it on the move until it burst with a loud bang and frightened him off leaving us to Telemark the remaining three miles unmolested.

One mile from our destination, we were struck by a blizzard.

My compatriots were equipped with wrist mounted satellite navigation devices however I was not as I had not attended the seventeen week course to qualify as a user of such equipment; and my navigation system was integrated into the Inflate-O-Mat® bed of nails currently languishing in an icy grave four miles away; but I did have a plastic coated map and a compass. However the "Compton's Hiker's Guide to the Mendips" was not really of much use when I was just two thousand kilometres south of the North Pole and the demagnetised needle on the compass did not improve matters either.

After three hours of wandering aimlessly around in almost zero visibility, I was, according to my map, just outside Draycott. I was about to set course for the Cheddar Gorge when Captain Arbuthnot, the intrepid leader of our troop of Specialised Hair Surfers, appeared out of the snowy murk and grabbed me by the arm and conveyed to me, by means of highly confusing semaphore which utilized a balaclava and a torch, that I should follow him and he lashed my wrist to his with a length of hemp twine from an Argentinian Pampas rider's bolas, a memento from the Falklands War, he told me later.

Within fifteen minutes by my calculation, but was in fact three, we were inside the underground complex. Whilst I had been rambling aimlessly around in a tight circle just fifteen metres from our target the Scandinavian Air Service had stormed Bessie's hideaway and, after a brief three hour exchange of small arms fire Ms MacTavish had succumbed to her own protective measures when she accidently triggered the halon fire extinguisher system in the coffee room in which she had barricaded herself along with several million Euros in small denominations, a stuffed Dalmatian pony, and a cauldron of her own subcutaneous fat which had been removed from her body by liposuction during her total body reformation. Unfortunately, once the haze from the extinguishers had cleared, there was no sign of the woman...Bessie was still at large (well not so large now; after the reconstructive surgery, but you know what I mean)!

Day 255

After returning from the frozen stretches of the Northern Russian Tundra by trekking south for two days and then being picked up by helicopter we debriefed at a now familiar airbase in Karup, Denmark.

Of Bessie, there was no sign; and, under the cover of the Halon cloud, she had managed to take most of the several million Euros with her too. We had, however managed to find the majority of the nefarious plots and demonic plans for the downfall of democracy as we know it which could have been perpetrated by the Brother's Slobodov had we not "removed" them, as Manning put it, from society.

Such plans as disrupting the entire internet base by inserting a single line of computer code which would type a random character when anybody typed in a search engine; imagine what would happen when Johnny or Jenny Teenager searched for the latest gossip on the varying inside leg measurement of their favourite reality star's pet ostrich, only to be directed to a page with a recipe for radish and sage soup? Chaos would ensue.

Another plan was to collect all the fifty pence pieces and file the corners off to make appear as ten pence pieces, thus undermining the whole budgetary reserve of the United Kingdom losing forty pence every time people used them in slot machines.

Total chaos.

A scheme too horrible to relate here, suffice to say that it involved half the world's resources of sticky tape, three Harrier Jump Jets and a box of Turkish delight and would have ensured that the quality of life of the entire human race would ever be the same again; but now, thankfully, would never be brought to fruition.

It was decided, much to my regret that Manning and I would return to Cuba where the entire assets of the Cigar Import Advisory could be employed to track Bessie down. The Society of Airedale Sexer's would be returning to Hereford to treat the injured (two troops had suffered slight rope burns in the chaos in the underground lair) and coil up the aforementioned ropes in neat rows to ready themselves for the next crisis.

The greatest joy was being re-united with my little menagerie of odd pets. Even Simone was pleased to see me and she playfully crawled only three baggage handlers into unconsciousness as they tried to place her in the specially designed transport crate. I also was in an ebullient disposition as I filled in my official mission report and in my lifted mood, I almost forgot to tick the box to ensure I did not receive any further information about investment opportunities from third parties.

Day 257

It was Napoleon Bonaparte that said "Impossible is a word to be found only in the dictionary of fools." So finding MacTavish must be a possibility even if we do not know where she is at the moment; or we are all fools.

The only way of tracing her is finding the large hoard of Euros that she spirited away in Russia, and I had an idea. Bessie is a vicious sexual predator who lives to torture her victims so what better use could she have for the vast fortune she has obtained than buying an large prison or fortress to carry on feeding her twisted desires? I ran the idea in front of Manning and he has committed resources unprecedented in Cigar Import Advisory's history.

So I sit here at my campers table with a computer that is so old some wag has scratched "Romans go Home!" on the plastic above the thirteen inch monitor, and while I wait for the fifteen minutes it takes for the computer to start, I flick idly through my 1957 edition of "Hutchinson's Illustrated Encyclopaedic Atlas for Boys and Girls" which is quite useful as the colonies of the British Empire are all marked in pink and only two areas; one on page fifteen depicting the tiny Islands of Polynesia and another on page twenty-eight showing Canada, are marked "Here be dragons!". On a small coffee table to the right stood my Inflate-O-Mat® Calculator disguised as a fifteen inch square Rubik's Cube and a pencil ingeniously camouflaged as a pen.

My PC finally climbed the slippery slope of processing and came to life, then I realised; a Commodore 64 probably didn't even know what the internet was, still, the screen cast a friendly green light onto the atlas so I left it on.

Modern Cuba!

But a thought has struck me as I sit here toying with a cassette of Manic Miner, if we place an advert selling a citadel as a unique investment property on a remote island somewhere, maybe she would take the bait?

Day 260

After three days of searching I think we have found our Island to set as a trap for Bessie.

It is called Mayaguana and lies 200 miles east of Cuba, 120 square miles and with just three small settlements on it; Abraham Settlement, Betsy Bay Settlement, (Which in the advert for the sale, we have called "Bessie Bay Settlement" as further enticement) and the quaintly named Pirate's Well Settlement, around one hundred dwellings in all. But most importantly, it has an old fortress overlooking the Caribbean Sea dating back to the days when Buccaneers roamed these waters.

The 'Citadel' boasts a stone built tower, where three cannon used to sit, and a fortress with several usable prison cells which should prove to be an irresistible draw to MacTavish given her proclivities; all for the bargain price of 3.5 million US dollars. We have received the news that MacTavish has taken the bait! Our Estate Agents; Turner-Round Briteyes, have just contacted us and have booked a viewing with my nemesis.

As I write this, Manning and I are travelling by motor cruiser to set a trap for Bessie at Fort Geare; named after a 16th-century English sailor, privateer and merchant, Sir Michael Geare who was the scourge of the Spanish in and around the Caribbean in the seventeenth century on board his ship Little John. We carry with us a plethora of gadgets and devices to enable us to take Bessie into custody, hopefully alive.

Manning has tried to explain at great lengths how most of them operate, but as a confirmed technophile I still have no idea what they do, apart from a device that has been fitted to Marty which will, by way of utilizing seventeen AAA batteries, a length of cat-gut and an array of foil milk bottle tops, turn him into a covert tracking device.

As we approach the Island we have been told, by way of a multi-band satellite radio receiver cunningly hidden in an Inflate-O-Mat® vintage Ormolu Clock that Bessie has been spotted arguing with officials in Nassau Airport, insisting that she is allowed to bring her seventy-five gallon vat of subcutaneous fat through customs as it is, ostensibly, 20% of her. Word has been passed via vintage clock to those officials to delay her as long as possible but to eventually allow her through intact as we are tracking the vat with Marty; his device having been pre-programmed with MacTavish's DNA profile.

I have also taken the extra precaution of placing myself into a large, and fairly uncomfortable, male chastity belt which was liberated from the Brothers Slobodov's museum of torture devices. As it affords the perfect protection from any number of perverted sexual assaults which could be attempted by Bessie I can live with the way the device painfully chafes my private parts, but I do wish that the Inflate-O-Mat® Seventeen Lever Padlock was not disguised as a badly bruised banana.

Day 261

Bessie flew from Nassau late yesterday afternoon on a small charter flight to the small airstrip which seem to be obligatory on all the islands in the Caribbean.

As she had never met Manning, he collected her from the strip while I readied my disguise for the tour of Fort Geare. As I glued my Inflate-O-Mat® Fidel Castro Fun Beard with added Inflate-O-Mat® Cuban Cigar into place I reflected on our preparations.

We had ensured that all except one of the prison cells were non-functional as she would probably insist that she check them out so we would show her the first one with the operational lock. Taking pleasure in the wonderful views of the Caribbean Sea on the top of the gun tower after a light seven course snack (which was heavily drugged), we would extol the virtues of living on a remote private island with no police force, and the fact that it would take a mere seven hundred and fifty thousand dollars to refurbish the property. Not forgetting to mention the clincher for the deal; the exclusive rights to a wooden beach hut and hurricane pit on Antigua.

Having secured my camouflage in place with only the one minor mistake of not inflating the Inflate-O-Mat® Fidel Castro Fun Beard with added Inflate-O-Mat® Cuban Cigar first which I put down to my nervousness; but the result did distort my face somewhat as I pumped it up. By the time it was done, I looked a bit like a bearded "Ugly Jake" who won the "Ugliest Man Named Jake Competition" of 1876 but was disqualified because he had paid "Mardy" Fred Blake tuppence to attack him about the head with a crowbar the night before the competition therefore forfeiting the two pound prize to "Not So Attractive Jake" the runner up (who had paid "Mardy" Fred Blake thruppence to attack him about the head with a crowbar two days before the competition).

I defied anybody to recognise me now!

I cannot begin to describe my trepidation as Manning brought the open topped Jeep to a halt at the front door of the fort.

There was Bessie.

To me she look a shadow of her former self; the last time I had seen her she only had half a face and weighed three times more than she appeared to now, the oil barrel containing her liposuctioned subcutaneous fat standing in the back of the Jeep was testament to that. Or, given that the barrel represented 20% of her old body mass, her slimmed down appearance must have been an illusion. Maybe it was the cloak.

In the half light of the cellars I felt a little more comfortable, but it was still extremely nerve-wracking being this close to both her and prison cells. I have not been that anxious since my thirteenth Birthday when my Great Aunt Daphne Caution-Howard insisted on kissing me on the lips several times as I had become "A fine little gentleman"; I can still taste the Drambuie.

I was commending the merits of the prison cells from within the first one when I heard a yelp from Manning and I spun around just in time to see that Bessie had produced a tube of the trusty "Strongo Super Glue®" ("Glue anything to anything, guaranteed!®") and had stuck the unfortunate Christopher to the Barrel that she had insisted he struggle down to the cellar with. Then I heard the sound I most dreaded in the world; the clanging shut of the cell door – I was a prisoner of Bessie once more!

My uncomfortable, male chastity belt was in danger of going rusty as the Inflate-O-Mat® Seventeen Lever Padlock disguised as a badly bruised banana was suddenly very moist.

Day 262

My fire-damaged inflatable Minion shuffled forward mumbling "I am not an animal, I am a man!" his disfigured arm thrust a gin and tonic toward me; then he began to deflate. I found that I could not move and had to watch helplessly as the drink spilled all over the floor and ran through the cracks in the slabs of the cell floor, with just a partially melted ice cube and a slice of lemon remaining on the stone surface, "Noooooooo!" I screamed voicelessly – then I woke up in a sweat.

I was still incarcerated in the only functioning cell of Fort Geare, trapped by Bessie MacTavish. My nightmare-filled dream had been my only form of respite from the terror I felt within. But fear is, I have been reliably informed in the past, a mind killer; and now was not the time to panic but to formulate an escape plan. I glanced at my male chastity belt under my shorts to ensure it was still in place; yes, and the Inflate-O-Mat® seventeen lever padlock was still secured.

That's when it struck me.

When Manning and I were preparing this very vault in Fort Geare, we had to overhaul this one cell and we had utilised the Inflate-O-Mat® Novelty Prison Bar Kit for it to appear as if it was functional, so all I needed to do was deflate the bars and I could escape!

I searched in vain for the discrete Inflate-O-Mat® inflation nipple which were somewhere on the bars, but to no avail; damn you Inflate-O-Mat®! Sometimes your products are just too good.

I reached into my back pocket of my shorts and grabbed the Inflate-O-Mat® Emergency clockwork chattering teeth which I placed against the bars. They only took twenty minutes to mechanically masticate their way into the Inflate-O-Mat® High Quality Vinyl (Guaranteed for five years) of which all their products are made. As the bars deflated and drooped forward to the floor I jumped over them.

I rushed to the stairs.

As I could hear no signs of anybody nearby, my main worries now were if Bessie had made her getaway and she had taken poor Christopher with her. My worries were partially unfounded, Bessie had made her getaway but Christopher was there in the foyer of the Fort. His unconscious form was a sorry picture; his shirt, which luckily was the only thing that had been super-glued to the barrel of subcutaneous fat, lay in tatters about him; of the barrel itself, there was no sign. His back was covered in contusions which looked as if Bessie had trampled on him several times before making her exit. As I bent over the prone Manning he moaned and began to regain consciousness. I passed him a bottle of cold fresh water from the nearby Inflate-O-Mat® Emergency Novelty Refrigerator and waiting until he was strong enough to stand and we made our way outside.

Christopher told me that it was only the brave and selfless actions of Marty that had saved him. The plucky primate had attacked Bessie with his pineapple spray while she was trying to put a pair of stiletto heeled shoes on and that had driven her out of the door before she could do more damage to Manning's back. But before she fled, she had grabbed the Inflate-O-Mat® Novelty Pet Carrier and trapped poor Marty within it and made her getaway with him!

Bessie had taken the open topped Jeep and presumably driven back to the airstrip. The only possible way for us to escape from the island and rescue Marty from that evil woman's clutches was to use the Inflate-O-Mat® Emergency Novelty Pirate Ship Pedalo which was moored at the small jetty a hundred yards away.

As we pedalled away from Mayaguana and headed North, I wondered how we would ever find and rescued my dear, brave little Marty; and would we be in time before Bessie did something unspeakable to him?

Day 265

We spent two and a half days adrift in the Northern Caribbean Sea on our Inflate-O-Mat® Emergency Novelty Pirate Ship Pedalo after it had shed two of its pedals and the rudder had deflated during a random attack by a shoal of barracuda who had obviously mistaken it for a Dover sole. We were picked up by a group of mercenary Opticians on their ship "Spooksaver", who had been commissioned to look for us by the Cigar Import Advisors.

The Captain, Greyson Austin; whose overt gayness shrieked at me all the way from his closely cropped hair to his bright pink trainers, informed me that if Marty still had just one of the seventeen AAA batteries, the length of cat-gut or any of the array of foil milk bottle tops which had turned him into a covert tracking device, he could be found with the advanced tracing system on board the "Spooksaver".

Manning was languishing in the medical bay with the Doctor, who appeared equally gay as the Captain, ministering all the aid he could whether poor Christopher wanted it or not. I was informed that the trip back to Cuba would take the best part of eight hours.

After only two hours, which had seemed like an interminable 130 minutes, Captain Austin informed me that Marty had been found washed up on a beach near Gibara and had been rushed to the nearest veterinary surgery for immediate aid. It appears that he had jumped from whatever vessel Bessie had made her getaway in and managed to swim to the nearest shore which, by happy fortune, had been Cuba, one little hand clutching the torn corner of a sea chart of the Northern Caribbean with some co-ordinates scribbled on it and in the other, a foil milk bottle top.

Good old Marty!

But I could not escape the fact that even a genetically altered monkey had better navigational skills than me. I also could not escape the guilt that I felt for getting my little primate into this mess in the first place. Guilt I had not felt so strongly since as a child of twelve, I had drank the Holy Water contained in a plastic bottle in the shape of the Madonna that my mother had brought all the way from Lourdes, and then refilled it from a dirty trough in the stables.

Day 267

We arrived in Gibara at around ten O'clock, just as the sun was sinking slowly below the crystal blue horizon and, as the clinic which was caring for Marty was closed, we booked into a small Hotel on the Ronda de la Marina.

There, during a liberal application of medicinal quality gin and tonic, Christopher told me what had happened to him. Bessie had surprised him with the sudden and gratuitous Strongo Super Glue® attack but had been able to prevent her from ripping off his shirt first which is why he only suffered having forty percent of the skin on his back adhere to the subcutaneous fat barrel. After MacTavish had secured me in the cell she had forced him at the point of a large plastic carton which once held Cornish Clotted Cream but was now full of drawing pins (one of Manning's most crippling phobias), to struggle back up the cellar stairs to the ground floor with the heavy barrel on his back.

Once there, she compelled him toward the open topped Jeep and made him climb into the back and place the barrel there. He had the forethought to use the height of the tailgate to lever the barrel from his shoulder blades where the glue had fastened the metal container. As he fell to the ground, Bessie became incensed and started to stamp on his back, screaming. She only stopped when Marty attacked her and, during the onslaught, when a plane flew overhead she panicked and assumed it was the Authorities (although it was just a local crop duster which had been chartered by the local crime boss, Vincent Dublin, to fly in a selection of thirty-five sacks containing highly questionable substances from Columbia); she grabbed Marty and fled in the Jeep. Christopher had managed to crawl into the foyer and passed out where I found him.

Yesterday morning I got a shock at the San Ramos Vetinaria; for not only was Marty waiting there, fretting in a small cage, but also

Cedric, my Lemon Toad. During my absence he had taken to staying in the kitchens of the Cuba headquarters of the Cigar Import Advisors watching Senora Abigail, the cook. She endured his presence because he made the kitchen smell fresh. Unfortunately, on the same day we were rescued and distracted by the news of our salvage, she inadvertently picked up Cedric instead of the proper lemon and started to grate him onto a freshly cooked Carp. Luckily Abigail noticed her mistake almost immediately so his injuries were only superficial.

So our plucky little band of friends are reunited and sitting on the terrace of a little hacienda just outside Havana. The fragment of map that Marty had liberated during his daring escape from the clutches of Bessie has proven to be fruitful; 46.32.50.64N and 08.06.48.40E, they are in Switzerland in the Alps, a mountain named Agassizhorn south of Grindelward in the Canton of Gom.

This means that we will have to make a huge sacrifice to get to MacTavish; Cedric would never survive those temperatures, so we will have no choice but to take the emergency lager supply.

Day 270

It was decided that we should have a few days off to recuperate, with Bessie ensconced in Switzerland and, with most of the known world after her, she would stay where she was for a while. After the last few weeks of remorseless action it was most welcome.

Christopher disappeared to indulge one of his more 'esoteric' hobbies involving three bungee cords of varying lengths, a plastic model aircraft, two goldfishes and a girl who rolls cigar leaves on her thighs. I think he called it 'philately' or something like that; I didn't hear it properly as he was rushing out of the door in a full length mackintosh at the time, which was a bit odd as we are not expecting any rain at all this week.

This left me at somewhat of a loose end. I spent the first day getting to know Simone, the slumber inducing Ocelot. She has to be kept in a different room separated from Marty as she is, like most animals, extremely allergic to him so she gets very lonely (Cedric, however, does not seem to be affected, although, as he is ostensibly a toad, he is covered in warts anyway so it is difficult to tell). I had only intended to spend a few hours with her but she kept playfully massaging my leg with her paws and I would fall asleep for a while. She has befriended my heat deformed Inflate-O-Mat® Novelty Minion and, as it cannot now be re-inflated I have let her keep it; it is so rewarding watching her cuddle up to it in her Inflate-O-Mat® Novelty Cat-Proof Basket and purr into sleep while the Minion makes little noises resembling flatulence.

On the second day I thought I would hone my self-defence capabilities as there was a possibility that I would end up facing Bessie alone and a little knowledge of hand to hand combat would be favourable. My Japanese instructor, Mr. Mano Iko, insisted that I first remove the male chastity belt fastened with the Inflate-O-Mat® Novelty

Seventeen Lever Padlock; this proved a little difficult as the small accident I suffered when incarcerated in the cell by Bessie had rusted the clasp on the belt. But Mr. Iko solved that particular problem with an oxy-acetylene kit and a simple four hour operation. They assured me at the hospital later that day that the scars should disappear in a few years.

Day 271

Whilst convalescing from my ordeal with the chastity belt I decided to take a slow walk through Havana. I say 'slow' because I was wearing an elaborate and complicated arrangement of bandaging around my nether regions that it appeared that I was wearing a large nappy. But, looking at the attire some of the Cuban youngsters were wearing once I went outside; I was quite 'hip'.

I waddled down a street simply called 23rd Avenue, which was crowded with locals and discovered a restaurant named 'Fresa Y Chocolate' (Strawberries and Chocolate) and gently sat in a chair outside perusing the mystifying choice of coffees that the menu presented, I ordered a "Columbian Late" and sat sipping it slowly. It was then I saw the reason for the crowds.

There was a flyer on the table advertising a procession by "Las Habanistas" who were, apparently, a famous *Ayuntamiento Soplador de hojas Formación de Marcha Equipo* (City Council Leaf Blower Formation Marching Team), who would be parading along with a Mariachi Band at eleven O'clock blowing the ceremonial paper leaf collection down the main road to rapturous applause.

But, as the way thing always seem to go, as the Band drew level to where I was seated, one of the petrol leaf blowers went wrong and blocked, the operative (not breaking stride for one moment) proceeded to hit it with his specialised "Leaf Blower Emergency Unblocker" or, as I would call it, a bloody big stick, and it cleared it with a "bang!". The resultant gust of pressurised hot air inflated my bandages and it blew me up and over the roof of 'Fresa Y Chocolate' before I could even taste the delightful dessert that it had been named for.

After crashing through the raffia enclosed roof of a nearby stables, I landed quite softly in a large clump of straw amongst a small herd of startled cattle who were destined for a local meat market. I hurriedly checked myself for injuries and was very surprised only to find just one small bruise developing between my thumb and forefinger of my left hand.

But not as surprised as when I saw my nose, lying on the floor across the stables and just about to be eaten by one of the cows.

Day 280

Yesterday morning I regained consciousness to find myself in a hospital bed in a large private ward in a Military Hospital, where, I do not know for sure; the nurses will only say it is 'Isolated'. They all have American accents so I surmise that I am somewhere in the Ex-colonies. My view through the window is obscured by a semi-opaque plastic coating with numerous air bubbles where it was applied to the glass in obvious haste. I can deduce, however, from the amount of sandy deposits that are transported on the medical staff's footwear that we are somewhere in a desert; my guess is Nevada.

When I awoke I had a huge bandage wrapped around my face with just slits left for my eyes. This was slowly removed by the lovely Doctor Eugene Unsworth-Fallsworthy, of the Unsworth-Fallsworthy's of Shropshire, with her gentle hands she then place a large semi-transparent protective mask on my face which gives the impression that I am a Super-hero who has not quite figured out yet what his alter-ego is going to be.

As she was treating me she explained what had happened.

I was discovered by Chuck, who had been tailing me all morning for my protection, lying unconscious sans nasal prominence and bleeding in the cow shed of the abattoir of 'Carne Fresca'. Following a frantic search by my saviour, my nose was found and, as the cows had only chewed it a little, he placed it (rather appropriately I thought) in a clean handkerchief. After some brilliant first aid from Chuck, I was transported to the headquarters of the Cigar Import Advisors where the only open medical facility they could find was the San Ramos Vetinaria where dear Marty and Cedric were taken. Senor Gomez Preperado, the head animal surgeon, placed me into a medically induced coma using a mixture of Rohypnol and floor bleach and performed a complicated emergency operation which lasted, I am told, several minutes; during that time he re-attached my nose and bandaged it, however the bruise between my thumb and forefinger took several hours of treatment by the repeated application of a balm. When the bandages were removed a few days later it was very quickly reasoned that the incompetent vet had placed my proboscis upside down; his excuse was that he was used to operating on animals which were normally lying the other way around.

It was then that the decision was taken by Christopher to pull out all the stops and transport me to where I was now. Dr Eugene informed me sadly that my nose had been almost unviable when I arrived, having fallen off in the C130 as it made a rough landing at the facilities airstrip when it clipped a buffalo that had been trying to graze on the sparse brush at the southern end of the runway. Ironically, the buffalo's own nose had been severed in the collision and it had been flown back to the San Ramos Vetinaria in Cuba as Senor Preperado had experience in that field of surgery now.

During the treatment of Cedric, the Vet had notice that the wounds the toad had suffered from the accidental grating of his back had healed very rapidly and Preperado had remarked on this to a member of the medical team of the Cigar Import Advisors. Cedric had then been secretly transported to the very medical facility where I was now for further study. A study which revealed that my little amphibious companion was not just a vital aid to cocktail recipes but, as the genetic manipulation performed to bring him into the world included the splicing of altered lizard DNA, was imbued with the ability to heal very quickly, even re-growing parts if required!

They had grafted a small section of his underbelly to what remained of my snout and reattached it to my face where, after just three days, my nose had regrown. It was, I was informed excitedly by Dr Eugene as she showed me the photographs of my Rhino-Bufonidae-oplasty, a medical miracle; I was just delighted that it was slightly smaller than the original and it was the right way up so I would not drown when it rained.

Another advantage was that everything seemed to smell so fresh now.

Day 283

I am progressing well with my convalescing and my new nose is healing well. It has, however, altered the reactions of my olfactory nerves which means that, aside from lemons, everything smells different so I am having to change my perceptions of smell.

It seems everything that once smelled nice to me does not anymore, strawberries, chocolate even cabbage boiling in water smell like varying degrees of rotting garbage and I won't even begin to describe what roses smell of, no matter what you call them.

But every cloud, as the saying goes.

I have discovered that the citric acid my nose now secretes instead of mucus produces an electrical current, rather like using a potato as a battery. By using a European two-pin plug, a length of wire and an adapter I can, having inserted the plug into my nostrils, trickle charge my laptop! That may prove useful.

Christopher has visited a few times to update me on Bessie. Apparently she has settled into a large mountain top Chateau, appropriately similar to the one in the film On Her Majesty's Secret Service Manning tells me. I say appropriately, not because I think of myself as a James Bond type character, but because Telly Savalas played the villain and then went on to play the detective 'Kojak' who sucked lollipops all day and that is what my bedpan now smells of to me.

The delightful Dr Eugene has informed me that I will be able to venture outside the hospital tomorrow, which will be a welcome change. I have so far only been allowed to wander the corridors of the John E. Wool Memorial Hospital, named after Brigadier General John E. Wool who was the oldest General to have served in the American Civil War according to the discrete bright red twelve foot plaque on the wall of the main entrance. I have spent my time visiting the sick and injured on the wards, but by far the most interesting ward is the "McGurgler Ward for Soldiers with Challenged Mental Capabilities", named after Sergeant Joseph T. McGurgler who spent the first four days of the American War of Independence trying to undermine Paul Revere's assertion that the British were coming by claiming that Revere was a "short-sighted idiot out for self-aggrandisement" and that he had not seen anybody from Great Britain, just a group of Indians dressed as Morris Dancers leaping around a maypole.

There on the ward I met Anderson.

First Lieutenant Anderson Anderson III had been serving on the Aircraft Carrier Foo King Huj (named after the famous battle in Hong Kong harbour in 1856 between an American frigate and a Chinese military junk) for two years when he began expressing the desire to place a private part of his anatomy into a carrot slicer in the galley. He expressed this desire over a period of six months until he finally capitulated to his fixation and performed the depraved act late one afternoon as the ship rounded the Cape of Good Hope. He was instantly hospitalised and sectioned for his own safety.

The carrot slicer was promoted, and she now has an office position in Fort Lauderdale.

Day 285

Yesterday I received some terrible news from Christopher Manning, who seemed to be in a state of shock as he told me.

Inflate-O-Mat® has gone bust.

The suitcase of inflatables stuffed beneath my hospital bed was the last of that fine institutes products, all the rest had been claimed by their creditors. I must admit to feeling a modicum of guilt by association because The Advisory did owe the company nearly eight million dollars for devices which had only been given to them on a trial basis to procure an endorsement.

All is not lost though; the remnants of that fine company have been acquired by a Japanese conglomerate and, as they cannot pronounce the name properly, they have changed the name to "Fuusen®" and they are sending out samples of their versions of the type of equipment we would normally use for comparison tests; sixteen tons of it in a shipping container arriving in Cuba next Tuesday. But given that the Japanese multinational in question has in the past produced items of somewhat dubious nature and skated along the borderline of copyright infringement, I do not hold out much hope for the effectiveness of this new paraphernalia.

On a higher note, I was allowed to venture outside today. Under the careful and watchful eye of Dr Eugene I spent a whole hour traversing the Hospital Gardens which, due to my new nose, unfortunately smelled like the garbage tip that they accidently threw the remains of Second Director Hector Nectar-Rivour on those many months ago.

During my sojourn in the gardens I could not help noticing that just beyond the hydrangea bushes was the main runway of the, as yet undisclosed, military base and on it sat a curious triangular silver craft which, presumably, was awaiting clearance for take-off. To see more clearly I feigned to approach the bushes to sniff the blossoms on it (they smelled of something akin to six week old soiled underwear). I watched with amazement as the craft did not accelerate down the runway as a conventional aircraft, but shot straight up and disappeared in an instant! I turned to Dr Eugene for an explanation by she made as if she had not seen anything, and as the mysterious flying machine had not made any noise and had moved so quickly I was willing to believe her.

Christopher informed me later, as I told him of the incident, that it was the first of the "samples" from Fuusen[*] and had been flown over from Tokyo that morning, it was made from a material that was so light that the Registered Trade Mark was heavier than the entire machine and tougher than the extensive team of lawyers who protected the Registered Trade Mark.

I expressed my doubts. Manning told me that all my questions would be answered tomorrow when I met Jeremy.

Day 287

I met Jeremy yesterday and I have to say he was not what I expected and neither was my reaction. I just wanted to punch him in the face from the moment I met him.

He was a short man of average appearance and somewhat twisted facial features, but I hated him from the minute Christopher opened the door to his room. He had an air about him that just made me need to mash my clenched hand right into his nose. I could not explain it. But Christopher could; and as Jeremy cowered behind a large armchair, he told me why I felt like this. Jeremy was from another planet. I kid you not!

I sat there slack jawed as Manning actually tried to get me to believe that this odious little man was a space alien. He claimed that Jeremy had crashed landed in Suffolk, England, in 1980 and having survived several severe beatings along the way and two assassination attempts in Ipswich before stowing away on board a container ship heading to New York from the Port of Felixstowe. Once he had passed through immigration as a refugee fleeing violence, and after three muggings at knife point and a vicious example of Police brutality, found himself claiming sanctuary in the Church of Inglorious Angels of 53rd Street in Manhattan. Special Agent, sorry, Monsignor, Eric Cappatoni contact his headquarters in Quantify, Ohio and was told to stop hitting Jeremy with the Cross of Our Lord at every given opportunity and that a security van with a cage to protect Jeremy from the three security vicars would be accompanying him to where we were now.

He had lived here at the hospital ever since, hiding for protection behind whatever furniture was available. The craft I had seen was a duplicate of the ship he crashed landed in East Anglia. As the technology on his planet was way in advance of ours, he had employed the engines from two old Delorean's and the electrical system from a

DeTomasso Pantera once owned by Elvis Presley, including the eight track stereo. The whole thing is powered by a complicated array of elastic bands and chewing gum.

The overwhelming urge to beat him to a pulp was a biological reaction caused by the fact that his alien body carries an extra chromosome which the doctors have categorised as 'z'. It triggers something within our bodies which effects the adrenal gland stimulating the "Fight" reaction. Almost feel sorry for the facially disfigured freak.

It was at that point the delightful Dr Eugene re-appeared and after throwing a plastic chair at Jeremy, took me back to my ward for my afternoon nasal examination.

Day 290

I cannot explain how excited I was to awake yesterday morning to find a letter addressed to me with your fine handwriting adorning the envelope. This was the first communication from you since my incarceration all those many months ago. My hands trembled with anticipation as I opened it using me new "Fuusen®" Inflatable Letter Opener, which I left slowly deflating on the side table as I unfolded your delicately written missive.

But once I had opened your communiqué and started to read, my joy vanished.

Thank you for following a delightful, but sadly antiquated, method of informing me of the rather abrupt ending of our engagement (which happened two day after my imprisonment, I might add), and your subsequent marriage to that balloon Viscount Albert Treadmill DePaul O.B.E. (short for OBESE, no doubt).

You graciously informed me that because I was cast 'Incommunicado' in darkest Central America and the scandal that my crimes have caused in the circles that we both moved in so freely, your father, Duke Darcy Abernathy IV (IV, apparently not because he is the fourth Duke, but because that is the way he prefers to have his sherry delivered into his puffy purulent body), decided to annul our forthcoming nuptials. His assertion of my alleged scurrilous deeds seem remarkably detailed as I myself do not even know why I was detained and flung into such a den of iniquity. I detect some underhandedness in all of this, by your mother Abigale no doubt (Gale by reason of her uncontrollable flatulence; I know she only has two dogs accompanying her at all times so she can blame them).

But I am not bitter.

I have, I admit, collapsed several times into uncontrollable sobs whilst crouching in a corner. I also admit to having visited Jeremy several times on compassionate grounds and beaten seven shades of whatever his little alien body excretes out of him. But now it is time to move on; I have decided to save my crushing disappointment, devastating feelings of self-doubt and the overwhelming desire to strangle stoats and coagulate them into a hatred filled, twisted and agonised revenge upon Bessie.

I have said my goodbyes to the delightful and tearful Dr Eugene and discharged myself from the John E. Wool Memorial Hospital and am returning with Manning to the ones who truly love me; Marty, Cedric and Simone, my mangled menagerie waiting for me in Cuba.

On the flight back I discovered that, despite very strange looks from our traditionally (so Christopher tells me) partially clad stewardess, if I stir my gin and tonic with my nose, it adds a refreshing sour edge to the drink, and then, after several more for scientific experiment, I found that by sticking a straw up one nostril had the same effect.

Apparently when we landed I only burbled your name eight hundred and forty-three times as they secured me to a gurney to take me to the Aleida March Memorial Clinic to dry out.

Day 292

I do not know why I am writing these records of my curious adventures as I have no-one to send them to any more, but as I have been scribbling for over several months now it has become a habit. Who knows, someone out there may find them amusing. And I will continue sending them to you in the hope that you will keep them as a record in case of anything happening to me, therefore I will just report the facts and not make any personal observations.

I arrived back in Cuba yesterday morning and spent the day with my menagerie; consumed most of the morning by trying to forlornly stop Marty and Simone almost killing each other attempting to be the closest to me. But it all calmed down and the rash on Simone tail should clear in a few days and Marty hopefully will wake up soon.

The container from "Fuusen®" Inflatables arrived whilst we were returning and we are now cataloguing the items. There are many intriguing objects but I still wonder at the quality of the materials used in the manufacture. A prime example is the "Fuusen®" Inflatable Pump, which is used to inflate all the other products; we cannot find how to fill it with air. The list also includes such innovative, but useless items such as:

The "Fuusen®" Inflatable Air Conditioning Unit who's "Fuusen®" Inflatable Heat exchange unit melts it after six minutes of running.

The "Fuusen®" Inflatable kettle, see above.

The "Fuusen®" Inflatable Bed of Nails, impossible to inflate because some bright Nipponese spark actually hammered the nails through from the inside of the lilo.

And not forgetting the "Fuusen®" Inflatable Bison Vacuum Cleaner which deflates itself the minute you switch it on.

Christopher and I have finished wading through the inventory of 7,656 "Fuusen®" Inflatable products and have whittled it down to a list of seven usable articles to take with us on our expedition to find and eliminate Bessie in Switzerland including a motorised ski bike which looks like a Killer Whale and a long range snipers rifle which, to all intents and purposes, appears as a sausage-shaped balloon depicting several Disney princesses.

Christopher has read your letter and he is keeping a watchful eye on me. He has suggested that we go out on the town tonight. Apparently there is a concert in a local cantina by a group of Guantanamo Bay detainees on day release, they are a thrash metal/ folk band who call themselves "Death Row Tull".

By the way, did you realise that your new husband was once held in a cell for three days in the mid 80's under suspicion of feeding the entrails of a beagle once used in medical experiments to a 67 year old nun?

Still, at least I'm not bitter.

Day 295

I spent two days thinking I was being followed. Christopher says I am paranoid: I believe that even if I am paranoid, it still does not mean I am not being shadowed.

Yesterday I was proved right. As I sat at "Fresa y Chocolate", I was approached by a strange looking girl of no more than twenty-five and dressed in only what I can describe, as a tree hugging hippy tie dye smock and open toed sandals. She told me that my apparent reputation as an animal liberator had made her travel to Cuba to seek me out to elicit my aid.

Her and her compatriots had formed an all British anti-animal cruelty commune which they had called 'Ani-mates'. They had discovered a laboratory deep in the Okefenokee Swamp which straddles the borders of Florida and Georgia (the name means "Shaking Water" in Itsate Creek Indian). There they continue secret experimentation on dogs for one of the tobacco industry giants. 'Ani-mates' were convinced that only I could help to rescue these poor creatures.

I do not know whether my boosted ego or the overwhelming horror after what I witnessed in Africa was to blame, but I agreed in an instant. I returned to the Cuban Cigar Advisory and collected a few items I thought I would need and placed Marty into his carrying case, muttered something to Eva Brown, the secretary, about needing a few days holiday (Christopher was out, and, judging by the fact of the gap on the coat rack, was expecting rain once more) and left.

"Sprout" to call her by her commune name (her real name was Daphne) took me to a small airfield just outside Havana where I met the leader of the group "Aubergine" (Cyril), he was an odious little man and I could not help wondering if he was not a crew member of Jeremy's spacecraft. But his intensions seemed honourable so I supressed the now familiar urges and we boarded the light aircraft for the hour long flight. Once we had landed we transferred to two swamp skimmers and I was told the plan.

The Mammoth Tobacco Co. had secretly opened an animal experimentation plant in the old buildings of a bankrupted Titanium Mining Company, who had not realized the outpouring of indignation at the environmental impact such a project would have in a National Park would actually go against them: the legal wrangling took months with TMC presenting the defence that they were "A Very, Very Big Corporation" and they could do what they wanted. MTC had re arranged the letters above the gate and moved in.

Aubergines plan was simple, Ani-mate would walk up to the front door and engage the staff in an argument concerning the validity and morality of animal experiments in this day and age. If that didn't work, Sprout would scream "Look! There's Brian May!" and in the ensuing scrum for pens and scraps of paper to get the famous Guitarists autograph, Ani-mate would sneak into the laboratory.

The plan did not start well, the security contingent had exactly the same reaction as I had had toward Cyril, but not having gone through the JAM (Jeremy Aversion through Manipulation) they proceeded to pummel Aubergine into a pulp. The other guards, being staunch Southern State Americans, had never heard of the guitar wielding professor of Astronomy and thought Sprout was referring to a box of matches and started searching for the fire extinguishers. I released Marty upon the Sentinels of Mammoth and climbed in through an open bathroom window.

I released thirty-seven Beagles and fourteen pipe smoking gibbons from the cells beneath the research facilities while the staff were having a cigarette break. I then placed my last Inflate-o-Mat® product in my collection: the Inflate-o-Mat® box of Novelty Groucho Marx Exploding Cigars which came complete with a now defunct guaranteed blast radius of three miles. I set the Fuusen® Inflatable Novelty Detonator for five minutes and ran toward the nearest fire exit. It was on the way toward the exit that I spotted a small puppy; it was a beagle and he could not have been more than a few months old; I could not leave him there, and as all the other animals had mercifully escaped and were making their way through the crocodile infested swamp to freedom, I picked him up and took him with me.

I made it to one of the skimmers with, I thought, minutes to spare but the Fuusen® Inflatable Novelty Detonator must have been slowly deflating and the rapid combustion of the Inflate-o-Mat® box of Novelty Groucho Marx Exploding Cigars was a tad premature. Thankfully, Marty was already waiting there for me and he jumped in his box without even noticing the puppy. We sped back through the swamp toward the airstrip where we waited for over three hours for the others, but no one turned up; so with a heavy heart we flew back to Cuba.

I have decided to keep the puppy, it will be company for Simone once he has completed the course of nicotine-substitute patches and sprays; I'm going to call him Darwin.

By the way, I was looking through some old family documents and discovered that one of your spouse's Great Great Uncle's was deported to the Antipodes for dubious sexual advances toward the Princess Victoria armed with two Cos lettuces and a haddock. I hope you realise what sort of family you have married into.

Still, I'm not bitter.

Day 300

Christopher and I left Havana by boat three days ago for Fort Lauderdale where we went through our final preparations for our mission to find Bessie.

We had to leave Cedric and Simone behind (Simone did not care, she has Darwin to look after now; her maternal side kicked in as soon as I introduced them to each other; despite of her being an Ocelot and him being a dog.), but Marty was determined to come with me and clung onto me for dear life so I had no choice there. I think he wants to see Bessie meet her demise as much as I do.

All the intelligence reports indicated that she had taken advantage of the last few weeks and securely ensconced herself within her mountain top stronghold in Switzerland. The plan was to swoop in by helicopters with the same covert military "black" squad that we went into action with in Russia, secure the Citadel and take Bessie into 'custody' with extreme prejudice.

We flew into Aeroporto Ambri with the Italian Authorities blessing on a C130 Hercules transport plane and from there transferred ourselves and all our equipment to two Blackhawk helicopters. Before we left on the mission, Marty had been presented with a miniature Navy SEAL tactical overalls, complete with insignia and an honorary rank of sergeant. In return I had taught him to salute. Whilst I dressed Marty in his new uniform, Christopher checked our equipment one last time. I still had my doubts about the reliability of "Fuusen®" products.

And how right I was to harbour those doubts.

We swept onto the roof of Bessie's Citadel on the top of the Agazzihorn Mountain just as the sun was setting behind the Bernese Alps bathing the mountain top in orange and glinting off the huge Aletsch Glacier in the distance. God it was cold and it had started snowing the minute we were in the air. I was fastening my "Fuusen®"

Novelty Inflatable Night Vision Goggles which were easily integrated with the "Fuusen®" Novelty Inflatable Comedy Breathing Apparatus and the "Fuusen®" Novelty Inflatable personal communication device (earphones designed as two pink daisies and a microphone in the shape of a spring onion), when the word came through that the mission was a go.

The roof of Bastion Bessie was covered in a thick layer of snow and was almost impenetrable but for a wooden hatch which I found by falling over it and landing face first in the white blanket deposited on the rooftop. While I struggled to get back to my feet, Christopher deployed the "Fuusen®" Novelty Inflatable Chain Saw but it sprung a leak almost instantly so it was thrown to one side with the also defunct "Fuusen®" Novelty Inflatable snow blower. I was struggling to remove my "Fuusen®" Novelty Inflatable paraphernalia as they had all burst under the impact of my head with the tiles on the roof. Marty solved the problem by showing us all with great delight and a salute, that there was no lock on the hatch.

Captain Arbuthnot, the intrepid leader of our troop was the first to clamber down the narrow channel leading down into the dark interior. I was about to follow when Christopher barged past me and rapidly descended into the unknown he seemed even more keen than me to facilitate the capture of MacTavish! I took a deep breath and followed.

After a climb which seemed to last hours but was actually only a few minutes I was standing at the bottom of the ladder with the Captain in total shock staring at the twisted dead body of my compatriot and friend Christopher Denzel Manning.

Poor Manning had donned his "Fuusen®" Novelty Inflatable Sudden Impact Safety Air Bag when we had deployed from the helicopter to the roof; nobody was sure whether he had accidentally triggered the device as he struggled with the "Fuusen®" Novelty Inflatable Chain Saw or it was the inferior cost-cutting manufacture of the product which had caused it to misfire. But it explosively inflated just after he had put it on and one of the seams ruptured under the strain of the compressed air which had propelled him past me and down the shaft. He had smashed fatally into the concrete at Arbuthnot's feet, but at least his death had been quick but very painful as the Captain described the noise Manning's head had made as it made contact with every tread of the metal ladder on the way down. Poor Christopher, unlike the rungs I will miss him.

But now that meant that I was in charge of the mission!

Heaven help us all.

Day 301

We moved Christopher's remains back up to the roof and buried it in the snow to wait until we came back. The Captain and I waited below, but we were trying not to laugh. Manning's "Fuusen®" Novelty Inflatable Sudden Impact Safety Air Bag had not fully deflated and it made rather embarrassing sounds as his body struck the occasional rung of the ladder as it was hauled back up the shaft to his temporary resting place. It was exacerbated by Sergeant Devlin O'Neill shouting "Sorry!" from the roof every time there was a noise.

The rest of the squad joined us after securing Manning's body and we started the search for Bessie.

The shaft had brought us to the cellar of the house undetected so far; we had expected an array of electronic countermeasures but there were none, which was a relief as the only gear we had to overcome them had been in the unfortunate Christopher's backpack and that now had a hole in it. Marty had gone ahead to scout for guard dogs and the like whilst we had been taking care of Manning's corpse and now we could hear whimpering up ahead as we crept down the only and dimly lit corridor.

We found Marty sitting astride a large Rottweiler which now was covered in that nasty looking rash that only my pineapple marmoset could inflict on any animal who had the misfortune to encounter him. I patted him on the head and he climbed up onto my shoulder. There was a heavily fortified door ahead of us and Captain Arbuthnot employed a crowbar and broke the padlock and we went through and up some stairs to the next level.

It was the now almost familiar MacTavish trademark of cells, six of them and four were occupied; all prisoners were wearing an assortment of skiing gear; from anoraks to elaborately pattern polo necked sweaters in various states of repair but not one of them were wearing pants, all of the men had haunted looks upon their faces and only two of them actually responded to our appearance. I followed the captain upward with a shudder imagining what these poor souls had experienced.

We burst through the next door into the main building in time to see Bessie running out of the rear door of the kitchen toward a snow-cat. We followed at full run, Sergeant O'Neill opened fire and sprayed the Cat with gunshot but Bessie made it into the cabin and started the tracked vehicle and engaged the gears and started to drive off. O'Neill's spray of bullets had however damaged on of the tracks and it just sprung open as she moved off, the vehicle spun to the right and fell over the snow covered side of the mountain. Bessie pressed her hands against the windscreen as if to push herself away from the slope, but the whole thing just slipped out of sight; the look of terror on her face was almost worth the torture she had extracted in her past.

Captain Arbuthnot looked over the edge and pronounced that no-one could have survived the plummet, but we would check it out once we had released the prisoners. I returned somewhat in shock; in the past twenty-five minutes I had lost both my best friend and my worst enemy. Only half interested I looked around the kitchen for clues as to what Bessie had been doing before we burst in on her. It would appear that she had been cooking. A recipe book written in her scrawling hand lay open on the worktop and ingredients were littered about it too. It seemed like she was making a pudding using various grains and chicken mixed with egg

Ah well, the best made flans of rice and hens and all that.

Day 304

After we had loaded the mortal remains of Christopher on board Captain Arbuthnot and I jumped into the first Black Hawk and instructed the pilot to descend to where the Sno-cat had smashed in to the mountainside. He expertly landed the helicopter on the flat icy outcrop that Bessie's machine had come to its sudden stop and he joined us in the hunt for her remains. We searched in vain for over an hour but there was no sign of MacTavish at all, had she just slipped over the edge to lie at the bottom of the Alpen abyss? Or had fate once again stepped in and saved her?

After a short conversation we came to the decision that we would return to the rest of the team, there we would send them back to base with Manning's remains and then we would do a sweep of the 24 kilometre long Aletsch Glacier which passed the base of the Agazzihorn.

We were half way through the reconnaissance when Marty started to get very agitated in his pet carrier which awoke Arbuthnot who had been displaying the ability that all servicemen seem to have; that of falling asleep whenever they could. I released my diminutive pineapple marmoset and he jumped onto my shoulder and started to screech loudly at the tarpaulin under which we had placed the dearly departed Christopher before we moved him. As I examined the covering from where we sat in the gloom of the helicopter I could see two glowing points of light burning bright beneath the corner of the sheet. My first thought was that it was a tiger, then I chastised myself; what would a tiger be doing in Switzerland? Besides which, to the best of my knowledge tigers do not even like flying.

Whilst I was still pondering this apparent quandary, the canvas was thrown aside and Bessie MacTavish herself rose up from the floor!

Arbuthnot was closer to her than I was, but before he could react she pushed him out of the open door of the Black Hawk and he landed, most fortunately for him, in a large snow drift in one of the crevices of the glacier. Marty leapt at her spraying his citrus ejection straight at her face but to little consequence as she was wearing snow goggles which was the source of the reflection that we had seen under the canvas. Bessie knocked aside Marty with one swift blow of her arm and he landed in a tiny heap in the corner of the deck.

I am not a person who loses his temper very much, but I saw red then; no one attacks my little friend!

I leapt at MacTavish and attacked her with my "Fuusen®" Inflatable Novelty Pizza Cutter which I had next to me as a precaution; it had little effect as it deflated on contact with her head. Luckily I still had the last Inflate-O-Mat® Inflatable Novelty Maniacal Sexual Predator Subduing Mallet (including the new improved "Mallard" squeaker) in existence and, under a rain of blows and quacks I forced her back toward the door she had so incautiously hurled the Captain through. In response she produced a large hat pin with "Welcome to Skegness!" engraved on the end and pierced my mallet.

The pilot, Flight Lieutenant Adrian Chinless-Smythe of the Gloucestershire Chinless-Smythe's, custodians of the alternative Magna Carter (the one where King John had signed his name as "Sir Michael of Mouse" in a last ditch attempt to foil the Lords at Runnymede, thus starting the tradition which can be seen, even today, in Guest Books across the globe), realised what was occurring and threw the helicopter into a vertical climb at a high rate of knots which threw both Bessie and myself toward the tail section. I smashed into the large metal barrel in which MacTavish had her subcutaneous fat that she had managed to sneak onto the aircraft (as much as I hate her, you have to admire the strength and tenacity of the woman), and I lost consciousness.

When I regained my senses, I found myself in a life raft drifting like so much flotsam toward a sandy beach on which there were people basking in the sunshine, the still unconscious form of Marty beside me.

I had no idea how we had got into the dinghy, I can only assume that the Flight Lieutenant had placed us there, but of him, the helicopter or Bessie there was no sign. Judging by the bright blue sky and the warm water I guessed we were somewhere in the Mediterranean Sea. Within a few minutes of paddling with my hands I had reached the shore, there I lifted Marty and revived him from a bottle of water that had been placed in the life raft.

As I comforted my little simian pal I was approached by one of the natives, a dark gentleman who did not appear overly curious about our appearance on the beach, but more intent on selling us a pair of sunglasses and a battery operated dancing Friesian cow. I pushed him away and stood, Marty took his usual place on my shoulder and we made our way up the beach.

I could hear the thumping rhythm of some strange beat emanating from a series of building set away from the shore and decided to investigate. Several times I had to brush away people who seemed intent on me taking photographs of them with Marty, until I reached the source of the music; I was not prepared for the sight that met my eyes.

It appeared to be a bar. It was dark but with bright flashing lights and tracks of lasers beam reflected off a rotating mirror ball set in the ceiling. The floor was packed with youngsters weaving and gyrating frantically to the beat that I had heard from the shoreline. The smell, even to my lemon enhanced hooter was overwhelming; a mixture of Tequila, Sun Screen and vomit. It was then I realised where we had washed up.

We were in Magalluf!

Marty and I have been here two days now, I am able to raise enough money to survive by charging three Euros a time for people to have their picture taken with Marty as they had been trying to do when we first arrived. It has enabled us to rent a cheap room in a hostel and to eat. Even though it has only been two days it seems an eternity;

every night around ten O'clock the streets fill with rowdy drunk and abusive crowds who shout insults at each other, fight and throw up in the streets. Then, once the Police and Taxi drivers go home, the holiday makers come out to play.

I have formulated a theory of how Mallorca was formed.

Thousands of years ago, when the Ancient Greeks started to explore their surrounds by setting sail in their Galleys they forgot one thing; an effective sewage disposal system for their boats. Therefore the lower decks of their ships would become quickly filled with effluent and even before they had got anywhere near the Straits of Gibraltar their craft would be in danger of sinking under the added weight of the sewage; so they would stop and shovel their waste overboard. Over hundreds of years this formed a large heap which eventually became the Balearic Islands.

Over the last year I have been almost killed several times by a deviant sexual predator, shot at and sunk by the French Navy and almost lynched by a crowd of itinerant Hispanic prisoners; but none of that compares to here.

I have to get away from this place....But how?

I have also discovered that your husband's next door neighbour's auntie's best friend once looked at a copy of a magazine from the top shelf in Smiths. This is the type of social circle your marital family move within.

Still, I am not bitter.

The Curious Adventures of Christopher Carrick-Bentley will continue soon..............

If you enjoyed this, why not
consider one of these titles from
B S DAVIES
<u>A LIFE FOR INFINITE ENJOYMENT</u>[1]
<u>GOLDEN GROVE</u>[2]
<u>DARKNESS FALLS</u>[3]
<u>Visit the website</u>[4]

---

1. https://www.smashwords.com/books/view/710088

2. https://www.smashwords.com/books/view/710128

3. https://www.smashwords.com/books/view/710132

4. http://mybookshop.000webhostapp.com